JOURNEYING TOGETHER

A Bishop's Charges to his Pilgrim People

JOURNEYING TOGETHER
A Bishop's Charges to his Pilgrim People

Rev. Dr. Daniel S. Thiagarajah
Bishop of Church of South India, Jaffna Diocese

Editor
John Bottomley

2020

Journeying Together: A Bishop's Charges to his Pilgrim People –
Published by the Indian Society for Promoting Christian Knowledge
(ISPCK), Post Box 1585, Kashmere Gate, Delhi-110006.

ISBN: 978-93-88945-65-3

Cover photo credit: Margaret Neith

Laser typeset by

ISPCK, Post Box 1585, 1654, Madarsa Road, Kashmere Gate,
Delhi-110006 • *Tel:* 23866323

e-mail: ashish@ispck.org.in • ella@ispck.org.in
website: www.ispck.org.in

Printed at Saurabh Printers, Noida.

For Gunalan Thiagarajah,

beloved brother,

And all the saints of Jaffna Diocese

Who sustained me at all times

And by God's grace still journey with me.

Contents

Introduction

This is a collection of the charges given by me as Bishop to my Diocesan Council over a period of thirteen years. Each address comprises two elements: the charge is partly contextual theology and partly, preaching. The charges reflect my personal struggle to make theological sense of the dramatic upheavals, conflicts and violence in our Sri Lankan context - from civil war and the anguish of schism, to post-war trauma and suffering, the personal trial of an attempted assassination, to our renewal as a national church of reconciliation, and then the struggle for reconstruction of church and nation. I have also offered the Council a vision of, and a calling to what Christ may be requiring of us as individuals and as a Council. At times, I also witness to my experience of Christ's presence with me in times of sorrow and joy.

When you read these charges to my Council as their Bishop, perhaps you will wonder - as I have - whether all contextual theology needs to be, in part, preaching, and whether all preaching needs to be, in part, contextual theology. Some of my pastors and lay people think doing theology is something that only academics do, but I believe the discipline of theology helps me to read 'the signs of the times'. In turn this equips me to preach a gospel that addresses the context in which our lives and our church are seeking to follow our Lord's good news of liberation and mercy. At least for me, the privilege of offering a Bishop's charge for each Diocesan Council is an aspect of the journey we have shared together as a Council that has afforded me the opportunity to integrate these two dimensions of my vocation, which I hold as a blessing.

Bringing the charges together in this collection places on record the struggles facing our Diocese in this tumultuous period of Sri Lanka's history and the history of the Church of South India. I was recently asked by a man from another country about what publications I could suggest he might study to learn more of the church's history in Sri Lanka. It occurred to me that one consequence of the upheaval due to our long-running civil war has been the destruction of so many of our historical records, and the disruption of academic study of important aspects of church and national life. I trust that this small collection is a helpful contribution to rebuilding the historical record of Sri Lanka's churches.

The charges cover the period from my first Diocesan Council in 2007 to my final meeting with the Council in 2019, three years prior to my retirement as Bishop of Jaffna Diocese, Church of South India. I am grateful to Rev. John Bottomley for his careful editing of the text and his oversight of the project to bring it to fruition. My thanks also to Rev. Dr. Ashish Amos, General Secretary and Mrs. Ella Sonawane, Associate General Secretary of the Indian Society for Promoting Christian Knowledge (ISPCK) for their gracious and professional encouragement in preparing my manuscript for publication.

The Rt. Rev. Dr. Daniel S. Thiagarajah Ph.D.
Bishop of Church of South India in the Jaffna Diocese
Diocesan Centre, Vaddukoddai, Sri Lanka
2020

Journeying Together

59th Session: Jaffna Diocesan Council
of the Church of South India
2007

Introduction

Dear Sisters and Brothers in Christ,

It is with much humility and gratitude to God I am here this morning to present my first charge as Bishop of the Church of South India in the Jaffna Diocese. At the outset let me place on record my grateful thanks to the Officers of the Synod, the Most Reverend Doctor B.P. Sugandhar, the Moderator, the Rt. Rev. S. Vasantha Kumar, the Deputy Moderator, Dr Mrs. Pauline Sathiamurthy, the General Secretary and Dr Venugopal Kasturi, the Honorary Treasurer, and all members of the Executive Committee of the CSI Synod for the trust they had when they nominated, elected, appointed, consecrated and then installed me on August 21, 2006 as Bishop of the Church of South India in the Jaffna Diocese.

I thank those faithful people who attended my consecration, including the three Presbyters who presented me to the Moderator and participated in the laying on of hands with thirteen CSI bishops. As I present this first charge as Bishop I am also happy that those three viz. the Rev. S. Sawarimuttu Antany, Rev. Suppiah Thevaharan and Rev. Miss Daisy Aseerwatham are here with us today. I am indebted to all who said a prayer for me on that historic day.

I am happy that you are gathered here from the distant Wanni, the area between Vavuniya and Mannar, the Hill Country, the capital of Sri Lanka and from all over the Jaffna Peninsula, especially from the farthest Island of Delft, which gave a real boost to my ministry. I welcome you all to this august body. A special welcome to those who have come at our invitation to grace this beginning of a new chapter in the annals of Jaffna Diocese.

The chain of leadership

I am humbled to succeed three bishops of great caliber viz. Dr Sabapathy Kulandran who hailed from the Puritan tradition and ventured forth to cherish spirituality in its great heights, Dr D.J. Ambalavanar who with his prophetic imagination pioneered a praxis model of proclamation of the Gospel, and Dr Subramaniam Jebanesan who on the one hand both developed an ethos of Christian Tamil Literature and helped the community internalize the noble traditions of American missionaries who dedicated their lives for this soil. I am happy to have been associated with these three scholars.

My humble beginnings and inspirations

As I stand before you and give glory to God, I also pay my respects to my parents who dedicated me to the ministry of the Lord. I carry the name Daniel because of my father's great admiration for Dr D.T. Niles who baptized me. My middle name Selvaratnam demonstrates my father's friendship and association with the Ashram movement and particularly with 'Periannan' Sevak Selvaratnam. I am happy that I was consecrated on Ashram Day (21ˢᵗ August). I owe a great sense of gratitude to my mother Lydia Chellamma who sustained me with her constant prayers until she met the Lord face to face at the age of eighty. I thank my wife Thaya, my friend-philosopher-guide, and my daughter Lydia Gitanjali, my joy and my delight, for the encouragement they provided as I walked through all spheres of life with its many challenges. Last but not the least, I wish to place on record my deep thanks to all of you, my sincere friends, who journeyed together with me in all experiences of joy and sorrows.

History speaks for itself

Friends, this is the Diamond Jubilee year of the founding of our great church, the Church of South India. This is the 59ᵗʰ session of the Jaffna Diocesan Council of our Church. We are happy that we are part of one of the largest churches in the world. It is certainly a joy and privilege to be part of CSI that serves more than 4 million people in 22 dioceses in four States in India and throughout Sri Lanka through 15,000 congregations with 3,000 men presbyters and 101 women presbyters. The Diamond Jubilee celebrations have already begun and they will culminate with a great event on the 27ᵗʰ September 2007 in Chennai at St. George's Cathedral, the place where the historic founding event took place 60 years ago.

The context that matters

As we gather we take to heart the theme appropriately chosen for our celebration and festivity, "Rejoice in Christ! Build Communities of Hope". Ms. Poorani Sathiamurthy, daughter of the General Secretary, has helped CSI by creating a meaningful logo that effectively captures the spirit of the Jubilee theme. The dominant symbol in the logo, the cross, closely resembles a light house that clearly conveys the message that the cross is the hope for the world. We rejoice in Christ because God has initiated God's salvific act in and through Christ.

I am reminded that in his *Confessions* VII.9 St. Augustine said, "In the Books of Platonists I read that in the beginning was the Word, and the Word was with God, and the Word was God. But what I do not read there is that the Word became flesh and dwelt among human beings." In the same way, he said, "I also read that he was in the form of God, did not regard equality with God as something to be exploited. But what I do not find there is that he emptied himself, taking the form of a slave." We are aware that the latter quote was based on St. Paul's letter to the Philippians, chapter 2 where he urges the community at Philippi to imitate Christ in their lives. He exhorts them to internalize the mind of Christ in order to live as friends and not as 'enemies of the cross of Christ.' (3^{18}) This is quite explicit if one continues to read chapter 3. As a conclusion Paul says, "Rejoice in Christ, and again I say Rejoice" (4^4). There is a connection between Christ's 'Incarnation' and 'kenosis' (the self-emptying of the Lord). God who longed for human fellowship sought it by pitching God's tent among humans in such a way God participated in human aspirations, struggles, agonies and sufferings. God's longing for human fellowship is well described in the Fourth Gospel, "I have come that they may have life and have it abundantly" (John 10^{10}). Life-giving intention of God who is Life was well demonstrated in God's giving of God's only Son Jesus Christ on the Cross. Without the cross there is no life! "When I am lifted up on the cross, I will draw all men (people) unto myself" (John 12^{32}). Hence, we rejoice in Christ with all of CSI in our Diamond Jubilee year.

Our pilgrimage together

As members of the Church of South India we have been on a journey, a pilgrimage. Our forefathers and mothers saw a great vision of unity in which divided denominations have 'died' to their separate identities in order to 'rise' again, to 'rise' together into a single, new and united church. This was exactly what Bishop Kulandran said when he delivered his first charge at that historic first session of the Jaffna Diocesan Council of the Church of South India on 25th October 1947 in Vaddukoddai. What he declared a 'New Chapter of Christian Church' necessarily implied the coming together of all churches that will bring joy to the Body of Christ. Indeed, there is no life or resurrection without death. There is no rising to new life without dying to the old.

We are called to a celebration that necessarily implies 'rejoicing.' It is a 'rejoicing in Christ' in order to internalize the will of God for us for the onward journey/pilgrimage. As the author of the Book of Hebrews says, "We are not among those who shrink back and so are lost, but among those who move forward and so are saved" (Heb. 10:39). So we are called to continue our journey in faith.

The theological basis

In the Book of Hebrews, the author makes an important assertion soon after chapter $10^{:39}$. The 11th chapter can be titled 'High praise of faith' because this chapter contains people of God who moved forward in their journey of faith amidst various trials, temptations, obstacles and turbulence. However, the author does not fail to say,

> 'Yet all these, though they were commended for their faith, did not receive what was promised, since God has provided something better so that they would not, apart from us, be made perfect' (Heb. $11^{:39}$).

With this in mind the author begins the next chapter, chapter 12,

> 'Therefore since we are surrounded with a great a cloud of witnesses, let us also lay aside every weight and the sin that weighs so closely, and let us run with perseverance the race that is set before us, looking to Jesus, the pioneer and perfecter of our faith, who for the sake of joy that was set before him endured the cross, disregarding its shame, and has taken his seat at the right hand of the throne of God' (Heb. 12$^{:1-2}$).

Christ has blazed the trail of faith. We are called to follow his footsteps. The Christ model is now introduced by the author, for he says,

> 'Consider him who endured such hostility against himself from sinners, so that you may not grow weary or lose heart' (Heb.12$^{:3}$).

Cross: a symbol of hope for the world and the notion of 'the pathos of God'

The cross is not ultimately a tragedy. It is a sign and hope for the victory of God's love overcoming human agony and suffering. The basic power to this affirmation is that the cross is not an isolated phenomenon but a key to the interpretation of human history. It is integrally related to all those struggles of humankind for the expression of a fuller humanity. It is important to understand the cross of Jesus as the basis of hope for God's mission of liberation of the oppressed and the disinherited in the society. Because Jesus' experienced the suffering, struggles and agony of humankind when he was subjected to the powers of humankind's evil and violence through his crucifixion, he becomes the symbol of God's victory over death and suffering through his resurrection by God's life-giving love. The crucified Christ is the hope of the hopeless. The cross of Christ fulfills the vision of the prophet Isaiah that the power of God is embodied in the most humble, weak and oppressed Suffering Servant. It is only because God suffers the weakness and suffering of the oppressed in solidarity with Jesus' unjust death that there can be hope for God's liberation.

It is pertinent to quote Rubem Alves,

> "Because God as the presence of the future, is the God in history, and since God's presence in history is always resisted by the powers of the old, God is a suffering God. There is no possible theodicy, no possible justification of what is by referring it to God. God is not the explanation of the pains of the world. On the contrary, God is the permanent power that denies the justice and right of suffering in history be being Himself the God who suffers" (*A Theology of Human Hope*, Corpus Books, NY. 1971, page 117).

Terrence E. Fretheim's *The Suffering of God: An Old Testament Perspective* (Fortress Press. USA. 1984) is a wonderful guide on the theme of 'Divine Suffering.' It may be hard if you have an image of an all-powerful God to imagine the notion of the pathos of God. However it is given much thought by those who experience suffering and injustice in the context of oppression and alienation. Fretheim gives three basic reasons for the divine suffering. First of all, God suffers because of people's rejection and crucifixion of Christ as Lord. Secondly, God suffers with all those who suffer injustice and oppression, and finally God suffers for the people.

Two alternative understandings or images of God are given by Fretheim, namely, the traditional 'monarchical' and the 'organismic' understandings. In the first one there is discontinuity between God and the world, where God is portrayed as being outside the world, as the one who controls that relationship. The second one shows the intimacy of the relationship. It is a relationship of reciprocity. Hence, the world is not only dependent upon God, rather, God is also dependent upon the world. It is a kind of dialectic. And because of this kind of reciprocity, God is also affected when the world is affected. God is affected in many ways by what happens in the world. Fretheim says that God is not untouched in heaven, nor are the heavens untouched. God's involvement in the world is such that God cannot but be affected by what happens in the world.

God's involvement in our world can be traced to the creation of the earth. Creation is the event in which God opens Godself up. God makes room within Godself in order to create something 'outside' God. God creates the world by letting God's world become and be in God's cosmos. The creation does not mean that God creates by calling something into existence. It is rather, God creates by 'making room' or by 'letting-be' or even by 'withdrawing Godself.' In a way, creation is the beginning of God's pathos. It is the beginning of the divine self-humiliation. Hence, we are called to believe in God's continuous creation process. Whenever we go through the experience of annihilation, destruction, alienation and death we are also given the assurance of God's re-creative activity that makes people alive.

The divine *kenosis* (emptying) is nothing but a clear proof of the identification of the divine suffering with the human suffering. God empties Godself. It is because of God's determination to be present in the world and with the people that God chooses to share and participate in human history. *Kenosis* is 'making room.' It is an act of hospitality. God is all powerful because God can be in solidarity and enter into our absolute human powerless. Through the act of 'making room' (*kenosis*), God's power for fullness of life (*plerosis*) is made evident. This is the hope for our suffering humanity. Humanity is assured that the negative in history is not a lonely voice for the simple reason God suffers with and for humanity. God negates human suffering by choosing to be in solidarity with us through God's own suffering.

Our theological position

Our theological position needs to be rooted where there is pain and human suffering, for there is the deepest agony of God and thus the deepest reality. It is apt to note what Fredrick Herzog said, 'theology must start where the pain is' (*Liberation Theology*, The Seabury Press, Inc., 1972, p.258). God is a suffering God. This is our hope because God is involved in a new task. God can change groaning into the cry of birth pangs and thus it becomes a creative force. Once again it is creation of new life and that is hope. Hence, we cannot speak about God without engagement (praxis) in human suffering and pain. When we take praxis seriously we understand that we know the truth in a different way.

The challenge of the times

Friends, it is needless to say how much our community has suffered in recent times. We have been displaced many times. We have learned to live without essential things for existence for we always struggled for meaningful selfhood and existence. However, we have also learned to live together in our struggles. We have been forced to think of the world from a new perspective. The theologian from Uruguay, Jean Luis Segundo expressed the view that the world should not be the way it is. What he implies is that the world needs a radical transformation. As we celebrate in Christ, rejoice in Christ for God's salvific acts, let us not stop as mere celebrators or people who only rejoice but make ourselves active participants in God's agenda for the world.

As we continue to journey together in the 60th year of founding of a great church let us take to heart that we are called to discern God's salvation:

- at work in the struggle for economic justice against the exploitation of people by people,

- in the struggle for human dignity against all political oppression by fellow citizens,

- in the struggle for solidarity against the alienation of person from person,

- in the struggle of hope against despair in day-to-day life.

Hence, our celebration necessarily calls for assignment. Our rejoicing demands our involvement. There lies a great task ahead of every one of us. We, as people of the Jaffna Diocese of the Church of South India, have gone through a variety of experiences. We have been forced to be dependent on others. 'Others' tried to say what 'we' should do. Our vulnerability due to war, displacements, political instability in the country and the vacuum that was prevalent in the diocese after the retirement of the third bishop was used by 'others' for their own advantages. We have been 'bent-over.' Are we not created in the image of God after God's likeness? Do the powerful have the final say? No, definitely not. Thank God we realized that what was shown was not what was there was in reality. Thank God that we were able to realize for ourselves that when 'they' told us what they saw we felt that we needed to know where they were standing as well as where we were standing and having our being. Let us continue to assert our 'status quo', which is only the image of God (*imago Dei*) to stand erect amidst all odds. Let us not succumb to enticement and temptations.

The Dioceses of Jaffna and Karnataka North were facing almost the same problem of Episcopal vacancy for a long period. In pursuance of the decision of the Working Committee of the Synod and as per the Constitution of the Church of South India, the Selection Boards for appointment of Bishops for these two Diocese have met and prayerfully selected the Bishops. The members of the Executive Committee of the Synod gave their approval for the process of consecration (As many as 58 for Jaffna and 56 for Karnataka North were received which was more than the minimum required for the subsequent process of consecration). The Executive Committee that met after the consecrations ratified the action in appointing and consecrating the Bishops and placed on record the appreciation for the prudence with which the Moderator and the Officers have acted in dealing with matters of these two Diocese. I sincerely thank the members of the Administrative Committee appointed by the Executive Committee of the CSI Synod and especially the Officers who helped the Diocese and the Bishop.

I invite you to focus your minds to the context in which I have been called to be a shepherd of this Diocese. It may be compared to that of the time when Nehemiah saw the need and was determined to rebuild the ethos of the people of God amidst all opposition from his own people. It was a temporary set back when I received the message of an Enjoining Order given *ex-parte* against my functioning as Bishop in Jaffna. When this was dismissed with costs another group of fourteen filed action but no order was given. Thank God, all cases were dismissed with costs. One of our clergy also filed action against the Selection Board and later against the consecration in the Courts in Chennai. There were also dismissed without any difficulty. Thus, the courts in India as well as in Sri Lanka have upheld the appointment of the fourth bishop for the JDCSI. I sincerely thank all devoted lawyers who spent much time in defense of the decision of the CSI Synod and all those who spent time in prayer for our Diocese and its Bishop. However, this series of litigations has prevented me from assuming my duties immediately. Of course, we have learned through what we have experienced over the period. I urge all of you to uphold the Diocese and its Bishop in your prayers. I appeal to all mission partners around the globe to help our Diocese to move forward with their assistance and support.

I am happy that I was able to discuss with our friends abroad during my visits and through my communications. They have assured their support to us for which we are grateful.

It is encouraging to re-read what St. Paul has asserted,

'We are putting no obstacle in anyone's way, so that no fault may be found with our ministry, but as servants of God we have commended ourselves in every way: through great endurance, in afflictions, hardships, calamities, beatings, imprisonments, riots, labors, sleepless nights, hunger; by purity, knowledge, patience, kindness, holiness of spirit, genuine love, truthful speech, and the power of God; with the weapons of righteousness for the right hand and for the left; in honor and dishonor, in ill repute and good repute. We are treated as imposters, and yet are true; as unknown, and yet are well known; as dying, and see – we are alive; as punished, and yet not killed; as sorrowful, yet always rejoicing; as poor, yet making many rich; as having nothing, and yet possessing everything.' (2 Corinthians 6:3-10).

As Ernst Kasemann said encouragingly in his *Jesus Means Freedom*, (Tubigen. 1968) 'For... what is decisive for all time is not how much we have believed, but that we have believed and followed him however little we understood about him.' So let us continue to have faith in the faithfulness of our Lord. Faith sustains a confident wandering. Hence we are encouraged to move in response to the summons of God.

We, as those who have undergone all these challenges, should never deviate from the task that lies ahead. We have realized that by the grace of God, our life did not end. So today we are encouraged to know that a new chapter has begun. God was turning our disaster into a new beginning. The assurance we have is that the one who asked us to get into the boat with him and sail off to the other side of the lake is the one who sustains us amidst the turbulent weather. We - as the community of faith - are surprised by grace when we feel or experience a new possibility. This newness is inexplicable. It is wrought by the inscrutable power and goodness of God. Of course this experience cannot be explained. Let us remember how the people of God experienced the wondrous works of God in their life when they thought everything was over. In awesome wonder they affirmed the dramatic turn of events that moved them from wretchedness to joy. They were surprised by joy that their God not only hears and answers expression of disorientation, but also resolves experiences of disorientation. We certainly were able to move from anxiety of disorientation to the stability and confidence of the new orientation. Does this not tell us of the intervening action of God to give life in a world where death seems to have the strongest way? Does this not demonstrate the decisive transformation made possible by this God who calls forth new life where none seems possible?

We are called to participate with our God in God's building up of communities that are voiceless, powerless, and are in pain. This is so evident when we read what is planned by the leaders of the CSI Synod for a meaningful celebration of the Diamond Jubilee. Let us make ourselves available to God and the world for the transformation of the world on behalf of the poor, for God is always found among the poor. Let us work with God in building 'the new heaven and the new earth.' Let us be prudent enough to hear the voice of God in the voice of the times.

- Let us celebrate the long existence of this great church in recognition of the diversity of humanity!

- Let us celebrate the unfading witness of this four million member church in recognition of the yearnings of grassroot people and people-based justice and peace initiatives that are a priority in today's context in Sri Lanka!

- Let us celebrate the fragrance of this united and uniting church that time cannot obliterate, in recognition of the human dignity and aspiration of fullness of life for all in the face of globalization that commodifies peoples' identities!

Come, let us join together in this celebration without deviating from the goal that has been set for us by our Lord and Saviour, who has left behind his footsteps which we should follow! Come let us give an account of the hope that is within us!

May the good Lord help us internalize God's will for us and for the world in and through us. May the Lord grant us true discernment to run the race with perseverance, looking at Jesus the pioneer and perfecter of our faith. May God bless all of us.

Re-build Hope

60th Session: Jaffna Diocesan Council
of the Church of South India
2009

Introduction

Friends in Christ,

I wish to welcome all of you to this 60th Session of the Jaffna Diocesan Council of the Church of South India. I thank God for this wonderful day where we are having almost a full house, which I believe is a miracle. When we met here two years ago, I delivered my charge as the 4th Bishop of the JDCSI, where I invited you to journey together being mindful of our greater calling. Indeed, all of us traveled together in seasons of joy as well as of hardships and troubles. However we have also experienced the great miracle of Pentecost repeating in this Diocese as we marched forward, trusting in the Lord who has called us. The One who called us continues to remain faithful and we are glad about it.

We are extremely happy that we, as a united and uniting church, have ventured forth in new areas of mission, new patterns of mission and new paradigms of mission as appropriate to the context. Our context demanded of us that we kept being in solidarity with the people who continued to suffer due to hardships of repeated displacements, loss of property, and death of loved ones.

Our context today is somewhat different from what it was when we were here in 2007. Many things have happened in the lives of our people. The geopolitics has changed to a great extent. Our people have suffered as a result of the ongoing and unresolved conflict that has been going on for years. To add to the misery of the people, the tsunami came and caused havoc in the lives of those who have traditionally lived along the coastal belt. Further displacements happened. The escalation of the war and the vast dimensions of it that unfolded also have taken people by surprise. Those who experienced displacement(s) began to experience a kind of 'uprootedness' in their lives. The last few months have seen much destruction, annihilation and loss, both of human beings and of properties. A community that has suffered much due to human-made war and violence was also affected from nature-made destruction that was unprecedented and unexpected.

Churches had to re-think their mission, but this combination of events made them go far back to what they were intending to do. Earlier we were focused on building of lives. What has happened over the past few months has made us re-focus on the ministry and mission of the Church. The traditional triangular pattern of mission as education, medical ministry and evangelization is today enhanced by notions of development and rehabilitation.

In the history of Christian missions in the 60s and 70s the theologies of liberation responded to two important challenges viz., endemic poverty and military dictatorship. When the theology of liberation gained acceptance in Africa and Asia, overcoming the impact of colonialism and addressing the issues, economic and social challenges were taken up, along with a new focus on the concept of development. That is, the end of colonialism on the one hand and the transition taking place from colonialism to independence on the other have propelled Christian mission into new ways to understand itself.

In the post-colonial era, the challenges posed by the people who have been 'no people' hitherto was now pertinent. Christian mission had to address its crisis of identity. What is emerging is that the important aspect of mission is churches determination to be in solidarity with the people, so that people's lives that have been at risk are to be supported by this liberative solidarity.

A new missiology

All this paved the way for a new missiology. It became necessary to think of the 'Nazareth Manifest' (Luke 4[:16-21]) rather than merely the "Great Commission' as recorded in Matthew 28.19-20. Christian mission was importantly focused on *missio Dei*, the mission of God as an intention for liberation, healing and justice. World events in the 1980s and 1990s became the context for everyone to address the issues of suffering and injustice that arose. Political oppression and war, civil unrest and conflicts have made the situation even worse than before.

Reconciliation, the notion for such a time like this

In this new context, the need for reconciliation also emerged. Churches were challenged to think and reflect on reconciliation theologically. Among the new paradigms for mission that were emerging, the paradigm of reconciliation was considered important and thought provoking, as it is biblically rooted and theologically sound for the enhancement of Christian faith.

However, a question arose whether reconciliation on its own was sufficient. Reconciliation had to do with coming to terms with a painful past, and engaging in the reconstruction of societies which had overcome political oppression or had seen the end of civil conflict. But theologically it seemed important for reconciliation to be linked with the need for liberation, as many communities and nations have longed to be liberated from the clutches of oppression.

Finding a theologically sound understanding of reconciliation

There are at least three understandings of reconciliation that come close to the genuine meaning of reconciliation but distort and even falsify its true meaning. These are:

> reconciliation as a hasty peace;
> reconciliation instead of liberation; and
> reconciliation as a managed process.

It needs to be recognized that reconciliation as a process takes time. Reconciliation is a process and a way of life with an eschatological horizon that cannot be foreshortened by circumventing history. It requires respecting, and often restoring the human dignity of the victims of violence.

Furthermore, reconciliation cannot occur without recognizing the sources of conflict and initiating a process that liberates the victims of violence from the structures of domination and oppression. The struggle against injustice is part of the genuine pursuit of reconciliation. Furthermore, reconciliation cannot be confused with conflict mediation, a process whose goal is to lessen conflict or to get the parties to accept and live with situations of conflict.

These calls want the victims of violence to let bygones be bygones and exercise a pale imitation of Christian forgiveness.

In trivializing and ignoring the history of suffering, the victims are forgotten and the causes of suffering are never uncovered, confronted, and resolved.

Reconciliation is not a hasty peace that tries to escape an examination of the causes of suffering. If the causes are not addressed, suffering is likely to continue and the wheel of violence keeps turning and more and more people get crushed.

Too often in the deliberation about peace and reconciliation the victimized are called to forgive and reconcile in a way that perpetuates rather than rectifies the root causes of injustice, alienation, and division. While reconciliation suggests a genuine change in relations, reconciliation can also mean a collapse into acceptance of the status quo because of a belief that nothing can be done.

Reconciliation involves a fundamental repair to human lives, especially to those who suffered. It requires restoring the dignity of the victims of violence.

Reconciliation contains four dimensions viz. political, economic, psycho-social, and spiritual. Christ did not merely announce the good news that the sick can be healed. He healed and in that act of healing proclaimed the Kingdom. Word and deed are one. They are inseparable. Reconciliation is central to the Gospel and one must be active in reconciling lives and proclaiming the good news.

> "If you take away the yoke, the pointing of the finger ... if you pour yourself out for the hungry and satisfy the desire of the afflicted ... your ancient ruins shall be rebuilt ... you shall be called the repairer of the breach, the restorer of paths to dwell." (Isaiah 58: 9-12).

The victims are often told to be peaceful in the sense of being passive and nice, and so they may be encouraged to allow themselves to be walked over. Others have talked about peace that was to be achieved by pounding the opposition into submission. Such peace is maintained by the rulers and the oppressors crushing the protest of the oppressed against their suffering of injustice.

Sometimes the call for reconciliation comes to the victims from the oppressors or the perpetrators of violence in the hope they will be spared punishment and the responsibility to change and transform the violent structures. Or sometimes the call for reconciliation comes from people who are outside the situation and have accepted the narrative of the lie, the lies about the situation of the victims perpetrated by those who have abused their power.

It is important not to give in to the lies and myths that were created either to demonize the victims or to conceal the appalling human cost they suffered. Victims of injustice cannot move to reconciliation if the truth about their human hurt and human hope is unknown. They have to find a redeeming narrative that restores truth. Hence it is important to see that the victims do not succumb to the erasure of memory of the suffering which took place in the past.

It is imperative to see that the notions of liberation and reconciliation are related to one another as paradigms of mission and that they are inseparable. Both depict the utmost commitment to the liberating faithfulness of God, and an acute analysis of social reality and the pursuit of justice.

Reconciliation inspires, guides, and shapes the involvement of the churches in societies ravaged by serious violations of human rights, divided by inter-ethnic conflicts and all manner of violence and injustice,

1. Reconciliation: being the work of God

Christians believe that salvation comes from God and not from their efforts. In thinking of reconciliation in that light, what becomes apparent, especially in social situations after conflict, is that the magnitude of the damage that has been done is ultimately beyond any human effort at correction. Only God has the perspective, which could ultimately sort everything out. Thus, Christians hold to the idea that it is God who brings about reconciliation, not them. We are but agents of God's activity, 'ambassadors for Christ's sake,' (2 Corinthians 5$^{:20}$) in the words of Paul.

For this reason, reconciliation is as much a spirituality for Christians as it is a strategy. It is only by living in communion with God that one can come to recognize the action of God toward reconciliation in the world. To assume that reconciliation is something that comes entirely from human beings results in the psychological and physical burnout so common among those who work in post-conflict situations.

2. The starting point of God's reconciling work: the victim

The common-sense understanding of reconciliation is that the wrongdoer repents of the wrongdoing and seeks the forgiveness of the victim. The victim forgives the wrongdoer and then there is reconciliation. The problem with this is that often the wrongdoer does not repent. Sometimes the wrongdoer believes that nothing has been done wrong. And in some instances the wrongdoer is no longer even present, and so cannot repent and seek forgiveness. The question that arises is whether the healing for the victim is dependent upon the wrongdoer and the wrongdoer's capacity to come to repentance! A Christian understanding would say "no."

In this version, God begins by healing the victim. This is done by restoring the humanity that has been wrested away from the victim in the act of wrongdoing. This is in line, first of all, with the Christian understanding of a God who looks out for the widow and the orphan, the stranger and the prisoner. The healing God works in the victim makes it sometimes possible for the victim to forgive the wrongdoer even before any repentance takes place. Not all victims are able to do this, nor should undue expectations be placed upon them. But we have to be able to account for the fact that such forgiveness can and does take place without any action by the wrongdoer. I believe that possibility reveals the very heart of the Christian understanding of reconciliation.

3. God makes of both the victim and the wrongdoer a 'new creation'

To be healed of the trauma of the deed, or to be forgiven for what one has perpetrated does not mean that things return to how they were before the conflict and the trauma arose. That would be to trivialize the extent of the damage which evil does. In both instances-healing and forgiveness-the victim and the wrongdoer find themselves in a new place, a place which they had not anticipated. Healing comes as a surprise.

Forgiveness is more than having the burden of the past lifted. This is the 'new creation' of which Paul speaks (2 Corinthians 5:17). For this reason, it is the perspective of the healed victim that provides the surest guide to reconstruction of a society after conflict. It provides a view which neither extrapolating from the past nor imagining the symmetrical opposite of the evil overcome can give.

4. The Christian places suffering inside the story of the suffering and death of Christ

Suffering is not of itself ennobling; by itself, it is destructive of the human person. It is only when that suffering is brought into a new social space and with wider relationships that it can become ennobling and even redemptive. For Christians, this is done by placing their suffering in that of Christ. This is captured in another Pauline text, Philippians $3^{:10}$, where Paul says that he wishes to know Christ and be conformed into the pattern of Christ's death, so that somehow he, too, might come to know the power of Christ's resurrection. It is trust in God's resurrection power - a power which is more than the opposite of death; a power which comes from the living God, not the crucified Jesus - that redeems human suffering from the destruction of an individual person or a society.

5. Full reconciliation will happen only when God is all in all

The hymns at the beginning of the Letters to the Ephesians and to the Colossians remind us that any reconciliation we now experience is not complete. God is still working it out in Christ. This understanding, coupled with the first point about reconciliation made above, reminds us that it is God who is at work. God is our hope, drawing us forward even when things look impossible by every count. This, I believe, is the vision of reconciliation which Christians bring to the larger discussion of reconciliation today.

What, then, is reconciliation?

Obviously, the rebuilding of a society after conflict involves many skills and points of view, including:

- Peace building

- Social and economic reconstruction

- Coming to terms with the past.

But importantly, reconciliation is not a strategy or a skill to be mastered, but rather something discovered - the power of God's grace welling up in one's life. It is a gift of God and a source of new life.

So what specifically do Christians contribute out of the perspective just sketched, and how does it function as a paradigm of mission?

There are two aspects of reconciliation as a paradigm of mission.

These are:

- Healing the trauma of the past, and

- The moral reconstruction of society.

No matter how much one wishes to look to the future, the horrors of the past yawn like a bottomless pit. Sometimes what has happened has never been truly recounted.

In any event, its full emotional and spiritual impact has not been plumbed. Without some measure of coming to terms with the past, the unhealed wounds will continue to fester, poisoning whatever new society is constructed, and posing the risk of victims themselves turning into oppressors of others.

What, concretely, is involved in the healing of the past?
Three things in particular can be named.

i.   Truth-telling

The basis for the healing of the past is truth-telling. There are four things to be noticed about truth-telling.

First of all, truth-telling consists of speaking aloud those things kept secret or hidden during the conflict. People were often not allowed to speak of the atrocities which they had witnessed. One could not raise the question of what had happened to loved ones taken away by the police or the armed forces. Speaking the truth breaks through the wall of silence imposed upon a society.

Secondly, truth-telling counters the falsehoods and lies perpetrated by the wrongdoers to legitimate their wrongdoing. Such truth-telling is essential to having a different kind of society. It also exonerates those who have lived under suspicion and false judgment

Thirdly, truth-telling is a matter of trying to establish just what did happen and why it happened. This is usually very difficult to ascertain, and in itself takes a long time. But without at least attempts at it, a society cannot construct a new narrative about itself. Hence the usefulness in some instances of Truth and Reconciliation Commissions.

Fourthly, truth-telling is an essential ingredient for the new society.

The very exercise of truth-telling becomes an important practice for the new society, something to be engaged in publicly and regularly.

> 'Justice is turned back and righteousness stands at a distance for truth stumbles in the public square and uprightness cannot enter. Truth is lacking and whoever turns from evil is despoiled. The Lord saw it and displeased him that there was no justice.' (Isaiah 59:14-15),

And

> 'because they mislead my people saying peace when there is no peace'. (Ezekiel 13:10)

To have peace we have to tell the truth - without truth telling, there can be no peace and no reconciliation. Further, I have tried to show that without justice there is no peace; even in the absence of open strife.

ii. The pursuit of justice

The truth must be told, and it must be acted upon. Pursuing justice is both a way of healing the past, and creating the practices which must undergird the new society. Truth-telling is a precondition for justice. To attempt to pursue justice without first establishing the truth runs the risk of seeking revenge under the guise of justice. And this is another form of falsehood, which only continues the violence of the past and does not overcome it.

Justice has two connotations. One is fairness, which is not sufficient for lasting peace. The other is observance of the divine law, righteousness. The state of being just before God is when the bonding force of love unifies the temporal and the spiritual. Then the task of the peacemaker is fulfilled. Peace has been established, justice reigns, and the outcome is reconciliation.

At the beginning of his ministry in the synagogue of Nazareth, Jesus, quoting the prophet Isaiah, proclaimed 'the acceptable year of the Lord' (Luke 4:19). The expression refers to the Jubilee year (Leviticus 25), which was to be celebrated by Israel in intervals of fifty years in order to redress injustice and oppression, and to recognize there are limits to the human claim on God's creation.

Basically, there are three forms of justice which must be pursued.

The first is punitive justice. This entails ascertaining wrongdoing and punishing those responsible for it. There is almost never total punitive justice; in the case of a civil war, for instance, not every combatant can be punished. The purpose of punitive justice, however, is to establish publicly that such behavior is wrong and will not be tolerated in the new society.

Second, there is restorative justice. To the extent possible, that which has been stolen is returned, those who have suffered loss are given some compensation to aid them in the times ahead. Often countries are impoverished after conflict, and the resources for the latter are not nearly adequate. Some public gestures in this direction, however, are important and necessary.

Third, there is structural justice. This is part of rebuilding society: the reallocating of resources so that the injustices which contributed to the conflict cannot be allowed to cause such violence again. Land redistribution, allocation of public monies for basic education, improving the status of minorities discriminated against are all examples of this. This final kind of justice is part of the long work of reconstruction. It is in many ways the most difficult form of justice, but also the most necessary.

iii. Healing of memories and forgiveness

The healing of memories and forgiveness are related to one another. Healing of memory does not mean forgetting. One can never forget what has been done, at the risk of losing one's own identity and integrity. Healing of memories means that the memories are no longer toxic; that is, they no longer control our lives and poison everything with which they come into contact. Forgiveness has to be understood in this context.

The first dimension of forgiveness is not forgetting; it is, rather, remembering in a different way. A victim of injustice is no longer controlled by the past event and by the perpetrator. One is able to see the perpetrator from a different angle. It may still be necessary that the perpetrator be punished or make restitution - that is to acknowledge the gravity of what has been done. But in forgiving, one establishes a different relationship to the perpetrator. One sees the perpetrator as a deeply wounded human being in need of healing. One does not have to become friends with the perpetrator; such may not be possible and is not always even desirable.

In forgiving, one seeks the redemption of the perpetrator. The healing of the trauma of the past is complex and complicated, requiring the efforts and talents of many different kinds of people. What the Christian brings to this process is concentration on these three areas of truth-telling, justice, and healing and forgiveness. What the Christian does is shaped by the understanding of reconciliation. In the now well-known words of Archbishop Desmond Tutu, 'there is no future without forgiveness'.

Without healing the trauma of past injustices, a society has no future. All it has is the constant repeating of a past it cannot escape. Christians engage this healing process because they believe that redemption is possible, and that only God is capacious enough to embrace the suffering which has occurred. They also believe the experience of healing that takes place in reconciliation is one of the most powerful experiences of the presence and action of God in the world which anyone can have. It is a concrete manifestation of the Good News.

The second aspect of reconciliation as a paradigm of mission is the moral reconstruction of society. It is important here to focus upon the *moral* reconstruction of society. This does not mean simply preaching that moral values be upheld. Rather, it means special attention is paid to the steps that are taken in the reconstruction of society. Thus, attending to the moral reconstruction of a society means also attending to the symbolic reconstruction of the society. What do our institutions, our policies, our actions say about us as a society?

Now the Christian Church cannot assume responsibility for the entire reconstruction of society; even if it embraces the majority of the population. It is an act of hubris to think the Church could do so. But it can have some say about the nature of what a society does. It can do this in its engagement in the public discourse about rebuilding the society, and also in very concrete ways. Let me name a few:

- The Church can create spaces of safety and trust in a society which has been unsafe and not trustworthy. In doing this, it creates an environment where the truth can be told, where healing can be sought. In creating these spaces, it also creates the social spaces where God's healing can be experienced. In a society which has been driven by hatred and mistrust, it can offer something for the rebuilding of the society.

- It can attend especially to the needs and interests of the victims. This is an outgrowth of the belief that God, too, begins with the victim in the healing process. In the competing voices bound to be heard in the process of reconstruction, it can be a voice for those whose voices are not heard.

- Most importantly, it can model the healing process, which the society itself needs. It can struggle to speak the truth about itself and its own role in the past, it can apologize, it can seek and extend forgiveness. This may be the most difficult thing for the Church to do personally, but it can be the most powerful form of witness.

- It can offer a larger vision of the healing process. If the story of the Exodus was the master narrative for theologies of liberation, then the master narrative of reconciliation and reconstruction is rebuilding the city. It can be the rebuilding of Jerusalem after the Babylonian Exile. It can be the building of the New Jerusalem, where the walls of enmity have been broken down, and strangers and aliens become fellow citizens in the household of God (cf. Ephesians 2$^{:12-20}$). The narratives offered from Christian faith may not be able to be adopted by the entire society, but it is important for any society to have such master narratives during a time of reconstruction. Such narratives allow one to see the bigger picture, and to not lose hope.

The moral reconstruction of society requires a sensitive moral compass, and commitment to honesty and humility. But precisely in those grand narratives of reconstruction, the Good News is communicated once again. The healing which can be wrought by God is on offer to those willing to seek it, and to live with its discipline. In this way the healing of memory and the moral reconstruction of society can be, in societies which need this badly, the form which the preaching of the Good News can address so many places around the world today.

A challenge for the times

We are called to rethink the Church's witness in terms of liberative solidarity. The Church proclaims and lives by the mystery of Christ. A holistic vision of the Gospel which overcomes all dichotomies – spiritual and material, personal and social, history and nature, sacred and secular – should be affirmed as the basis of God's freeing and creative act. God's liberative work is toward the strengthening and renewing of relationships among humans and between humans and nature. Life is sustained by inter-connectedness. Fragmentation and exclusiveness are ways of denying God's purpose for God's creation. Justice is the concrete direction of God's transforming and liberative work in our midst. To participate in the struggle for justice is to participate in God's mission.

We are called to understand that while we affirm the centrality of the struggle for justice in our mission we need to recognize that, in order to gain more justice, the powerless should have more power. At the same time, if the structure and orientation of newly gained power follows the same pattern as that of the dominant groups, then today's oppressed will turn into tomorrow's oppressors. History bears this out. Hence reconciliation is Jesus' way to avoid this. And this is integral to our proclamation of the good news.

Jesus' identification with the powerless was total and it is revealed on the cross. All who cry from the depths of suffering and despair will find an ally in Him. Jesus willingly surrendered himself to the will of God. Even in the darkness of human-instigated violence and state-sponsored crucifixion unto death, Jesus trusted God. Easter faith proclaims that God vindicated Jesus by raising him from the dead, thus declaring him to be the expression of God's own life and kingdom.

This is liberative solidarity that can re-orient our value systems and power constellations and usher in a new order. It is possible only if we enter into the life of others, especially their suffering, with openness and compassion.

Liberative solidarity implies embracing 'the Other'. It expects that we embrace others unconditionally in their irreducible difference. It is absolutely indiscriminate and strictly immutable. Those who respond to the 'otherness' of other people and, in Shakespeare's phrase, 'take upon themselves the mystery of things'[1],

---

[1] W. Shakespeare, *King Lear*, Act 5, scene 3.

will respond with the same sensitivity to other people's mess and muddle and take upon themselves their pain and anger.

There is no possibility to heal divisions, to overcome violence and contribute towards the creation of a culture of peace if one allows oneself to demonize others so that it results in the suppression of their irreducible differences, for example through ethnic cleansing, genocide, religious persecution, imprisonment, and various other acts of terror.

In an inescapably unjust and discordant world, the only hope that we have to attain a potential, tenuous convergence on what is just must be grounded on the will to embrace the other. If such a will does not exist, then each conflicting party will insist on the justness of its cause and will continue indeterminably in its violent conflict until the death or suppression of the other. The failure to embrace the other in their 'otherness' perpetuates violence and fragmentation in the name of justice. Grimly, there is sadly too much injustice when parties engage in an uncompromising struggle for justice.

The will to embrace and affirm the humanity of others despite their apparent irreducible differences provides the basis for discerning in them whatever is right or just in their causes and actions. Conversely, if exclusion becomes the basis for contact with the other, then primacy is given to whatever rightly or wrongly is named as unjust in them that does permit any positive relation with them.

The indiscriminate love for all does not, under any circumstances, imply that justice must be sacrificed or overlooked for the sake of peace. Quite the contrary. Peace demands that one be attentive to issues of justice, seeking to transform oppressive relationships into just relationships by contributing towards the creation of a genuine human community in an imperfect world of inescapable injustice. This cannot be done without hearing the cries of those whose humanity and dignity have been violently taken away by the destructive and violent forces of oppression. The process of reconciliation never comes to a closure, since all responses to collective atrocities and violence are incomplete and inescapably inadequate.

The churches in their solidarity with victims of injustice infuse upon those victims, as well as upon the perpetrators of violence, a new outlook on life that is grounded in God's love, which may liberate them both from their alienated state of being. This new outlook shapes the broader cultural habits and expectations that make peaceful solutions to situations of conflict possible.

Friends, we are called to give an account of the hope that is within us (1 Peter 3:15), as Peter has urged the suffering community near the end of the first century A.D. Our hope is in God who raised Jesus from death, thus providing new life for all. We are being led by the spirit of "Easter Faith" and we are called to be effective manifestations of that in a world that is broken by war and violence, in our context where day-to-day living has become a life and death issue.

What shall we say then? If God is with us, who can be against us? (Rom. 8:31) The God who gave the power to live in a broken world by His liberative solidarity is the God who calls us this morning to become ambassadors for Him. Let us take this to heart. Let us be moved by the challenge of showing liberative solidarity. We do not have any other option.

As we march forward into Province after Province we proclaim the good news of God which is 'LIFE' and 'LIFE IN ITS FULLNESS'. This is the message we take. The community is longing to be re-built. How do we do that? Let us first and foremost re-build hope, the hope of resurrection into life, life in its fullness. Let us be confident of the hope that is in us by our own acts of liberative solidarity.

May God bless us all.

Journey Toward Wholeness
61ˢᵗ Session: Jaffna Diocesan Council of the Church of South India
2011

Introduction

My dear Sisters and Brothers in Christ,

I welcome you to our 61ˢᵗ Diocesan Council Sessions. I sincerely appreciate your determination to attend this very important event in the life of this great Church. As you are well aware, participation at these sessions prepare all of us to view our greater calling and responsibilities in the life and mission of this historic church.

Most of you will recognize and remember when I became the fourth bishop of the Jaffna Diocese of the Church of South India (JDCSI) on the 21ˢᵗ August 2006 and presided over the first Council as the bishop. I brought to mind the great significance of the Church of South India and the historic legacy the forerunners the American Missionaries left for us. There in 2007 I called upon you all to 'Journey Together'. Then in 2009, I challenged us to get together to 'Re-build Hope', taking to heart the challenges of a 'Kairos' moment.

A new situation of extraordinary crisis

Now, two years since that Council, we gather to discern the will of God for us for the next biennium, 2011-2013. It is important to know that our situation is different today than it was then. A few months after we assembled then in this same hall, we went through a dark period. Our people have undergone untold hardship, tribulation, pain, anxiety and above all, unprecedented experiences of separation, loss and death. The aftermath of the war has created an extraordinary crisis through the large displacement of many hundreds of thousands of civilians. What shall we say then?

It may be pertinent that after two years since the tragic happenings, those who were in the Internally Displaced Peoples' (IDP) camps have mostly gone back to their own places. People are returning. Some have been resettled in their own lands. Others still wait to be settled. Quite a large number wait in patience to go back to their places of abode. But resettlement is not the end of their problems, indeed it may be the beginning of their problems. Those who get back to their homes have undergone stress, pain, loss and more. They are grieving the deaths of their loved ones, as well as the loss of their own belongings and properties. We should never forget that they come back into our midst as wounded people. So it is important we recognize what they really need may be more that resettlement.

While we give thanks to God for the ways in which God motivated us to be care-givers to such suffering people, we also take note of the heavy task that lies ahead of us. We are grateful that we have been empowered to stretch out our hands in small ways to accept and embrace our neighbors, these wounded people. We confess at times we have been complacent about what we did, almost succumbing to the temptation of self-satisfaction, self-boasting and self-justification. A spirit of 'heroism' has crept into our attitude.

On the other hand, there has often been a concern for truth and freedom. We have given voice to the truth about what has happened and what is still happening in the lives of these people. We have recognized that freedom for these people at various levels includes freedom from the state of 'victimhood.' However we have seldom realized that there is a third and important aspect connected to these two. This third factor is healing or wholeness, if you would like to understand it by the end result.

Healing and wholeness: a new imperative

There is a strong connection between freedom, truth and wholeness. Healing makes the connection with truth and freedom clearer. It's not enough to talk about freedom as if it is a hurdle that is overcome once and for all. We are only free to the extent that we are whole. And conversely, while our brokenness continues to be part of our present, we lack something of our truth and freedom as human beings created in the image of God's wholeness. Looking at it this way, wholeness becomes a vision, something gifted and to claim, as well as to aim for. The pursuit of wholeness for each other and our neighbors becomes an imperative for our Diocese.

Our Church is expected to discern the 'woundedness' of the people at large. The ones who return do not return to a place of Biblical promise, filled with milk and honey. They come back to a place destroyed, in ruins and filled with haunting memories. So bringing people back to their land or helping them with some relief will not in any way bring them a meaningful living, because their war woundedness is so severe that there may seem to be no end to their pain and suffering. Their haunted memories wait for an experience of healing. The movement from woundedness to wholeness needs to be facilitated. That is why it is important that we become 'wounded listeners'. When we do that, we who have also suffered become 'wounded listeners'. Then we are called to go a step further and become 'wounded healers'. This is our Church's calling - to see that our unobtrusive witness seeks only the dignity, healing and common good of those whose lives have been shattered and torn apart.

We, the JDCSI, are a movement. We have been moving ever since we understood our mission in a larger context. The first movement or journey took us into areas south of Elephant Pass in the year 1979, thirty-two years since the formation of the CSI. Then the Church stretched her arms into the greater parts of Vanni and Mannar, from Vavuniya to Uyilankulam via Cheddikulam. The third stage of this journey took us into the Eastern Province and then finally to the Central Hills. Our Diocese felt a deep sense of satisfaction with our journey spreading out. However the fact remained that we were a parochial Church, serving the Tamil people with the Tamil Workers, Pastors and Evangelists. Then came the 'shaking of the foundations' moment, when we journeyed together to the southern parts of the country to embrace our Singhalese brethren, thus becoming a national Church. While we are grateful for this unprecedented movement from parochialism to nationalism we must admit that it has also confronted us with new challenges. Our journey together in hope has shown us a greater cause.

Now, the challenge ahead of us is to discern the signs of the times. At one point it was to reach out and embrace those who were on the fringes of society. Later it was to find and explore ways of meaningful ecumenism, learning what the church is called to in being Church. But the most difficult question facing suffering humanity in Sri Lanka has not been answered by these movements.

The continued suffering in our nation brings us face-to-face with the question of human solidarity and togetherness. We are confronted with the momentous question of re-ordering human inter-relationships at all levels in justice and peace. Those who return to their own soil face many burning issues, such as non-acceptance, fear, trauma, especially post-traumatic stress disorder (PTSD), and above all their continued state of victimhood. For the wounded people who experience exclusion or isolation, the important question is that of inclusion or the creation of true communities where they will be equal partners; where they will have dignity and a voice. The hope of victims is not merely for economic development and advancement of technology but incorporation into new communities augmented by true signs of solidarity. Human solidarity is the most urgent question that needs to be answered. Any praxis or philosophy that goes against solidarity is one that jeopardizes the cause of the victims. We hear that the issue of whether they will be members of an authentic community of equals is the remaining unanswered question of war victims.

The *Missio Dei*: discerning the mission of God

JDCSI is a community in itself, often called a community of faith, but it is also a community bearing witness and living out its faith in the larger context of our nation. Our concern then is with the *Missio Dei*, the mission of God, which compels the mission of the Diocese to those outside our membership. This is the meaning of our community as Church. The healing sought by victims of violence and war is not to be limited to the community of faith that meets in a particular assembly. We seek our own healing as believers in a local assembly for Christ's sake, that we may bear testimony to and reach outside ourselves in order to bring that same healing to others. The kingdom of God, both as a gift and as a task, stands forth as the most comprehensive biblical expression for the goal of *Missio Dei*. Properly understood, the church is an instrument of the kingdom and an eschatological foretaste of it. The kingdom of God is not just a theological construct; it may be seen to be living in our context. In our context we see large number of widows, we come across small children without parents, and situations where the infrastructure of the people is completely shattered. In our context people do not have any means of existence, and countless limbless people struggle for their existence.

When the Diocese struggled to renovate and reconstruct church buildings we were confronted with the question if that was a priority. However we saw that broken people look to worship the Lord and to find some solace for their lives. It made us realize that the deep seated agony of hurt, destruction and nothingness should be overcome with meaningful and appropriate gestures of compassion for the children and women. We heard their need for reconstructed church centres that could accommodate these needy ones and provide empowerment and self-awareness programs. The young women are being helped with training for alternate ways of making a living. The children are nurtured in many Day Care and Child Care Centres. Health facilities and nutrition programs are being initiated. Job opportunities are being found to support at least a few families. We are happy that while we continue to do this we have also focused our minds on people physically challenged due to the war. From this we saw the vision to start the Centre for Holistic Healing (CHH). CHH is our response to the utmost challenge of these times.

We are motivated to have a mission of wholism (holism), community or shalom. Mission (or missions) has been rather preoccupied with word or deed. Churches have tended to define discipleship as either personal spiritual growth or a collective movement toward some sociological or moral ideal. Bishop Leslie Newbegin has said it is absurd to set word and deed, preaching and action, against each other. He believes the central reality is neither word nor act, but the total life of a community enabled by the Spirit to live in Christ. He goes on to say it is clear that action for justice and peace in the world is not something which is secondary, marginal to the central task of evangelism. Newbigin emphasizes that justice and peace belong to the heart of the matter.

God's imperative: a kingdom of shalom

God's imperative is that the church is to model and extend the reign and rule of Christ. It is a kingdom of shalom. The peace of shalom is more than only the absence of war. Formulated negatively, shalom includes the absence of alienation, material need, and oppression in society. Formulated positively, shalom indicates a state of comprehensive social harmony and material wellbeing in society. When we focus our minds on wounded people, we also need to look afresh of the task. Now we note the Greek term for 'wound' is the same as our English usage for not only physical wounds, but wounds of the heart, soul, mind, and social relationships. Shalom, in its Hebrew meanings mirrors the categories such as completeness (in number), safety, soundness (in body) [i.e. physical]; welfare, health, prosperity; peace, quiet, tranquility, contentment [i.e. emotional]; peace, friendship of human relationships [i.e. social] and with God especially in covenant relationship [i.e. volitional]; peace (from war).

The third line of the blessing in Book of Numbers 6:26 brings the blessing to a crescendo. The goal of God's blessing is summed up by the final word of the benediction, the Hebrew word 'shalom' or 'peace'. Shalom refers to more than simply the absence of conflict. It encompasses all of God's good gifts of health, prosperity, wellbeing, and salvation. This richly worded blessing comes at the end of the section in chapters 5-6 that is concerned about the holiness and well-being of the entire community. It highlights that God's ultimate will for all the people is blessing and peace. God is blessing the community, and the people are obediently and eagerly following his commands.

When we, the JDCSI, are involved in this aspect of mission in our war-ravaged context, we also realize that our mission has to be holistic in nature and character. Holism is a word derived from the Greek *holos*, meaning 'whole, complete'. Whether we spell it holism, or wholism, the meaning remains the same. Since the word has been co-opted in recent years by new-age philosophy there is confusion in some minds as to whether the use of the term implies a certain philosophy. The term is used broadly in anthropology, cosmology, theology, philosophy, psychology, biology, medicine, and sociology. The term is so widely used that it is necessary to clarify what it does mean. In missions, development projects are seen to be a holistic expression of the gospel, but often it is simply the juxtaposition of another element. The church program therefore suffers because in attempting to deal with the whole person, it ends up focusing upon one aspect or need and that aspect becomes the driving center of the program.

When being human is reduced to being a one-dimensional creature instead of a multi-dimensional one, human being is treated in the same way, for example, development is reduced to economic development. Holistic human development (educational, social, psychological, cultural, physical etc.) is not part of the development program. Medical care is limited to the part of the body which is not functioning well, as if it is a broken-down machine. So once again I like to focus on the meaning of shalom. We need to understand how shalom has been understood theologically by those applying it to life. Shalom, as the advent of the justice of God, communicates the sense of human welfare, health, and well-being in both spiritual and material aspects. Shalom is a way of life that characterizes the covenant relationship between God and his people. It is the best description of what the reign of God will be like: a place of safety, justice, and truth; a place of trust, inclusion, and love; a place of joy, happiness, and well-being.

Shalom occurs when people who are in a right relationship with God and each other enjoy share together the resources of the earth in ways that show Christ is Lord of all creation. The history of God's redemption in Christ starts with God's activity in dealing with the effects of sin. God's redemption in Christ is first about restoring the relationship between God and His people. Redemption is also about God's ownership and renewal of the whole world, or earth. God gives the world to His people so that we will be stewards of it.

Through God's activity in redemption, humankind is called to respond to that redemption. God loved His people with a redeeming love. Because of that love we are able to love God and others with love that guides our emotions; guides our social relationships; and guides the choices we make in how we use our physical energy and resources. Through the Bible, all creation helps us understand who God is and who we are in Christ. It is the Holy Spirit who works in every aspect of humankind to bring a response of faith in God's redeeming love…emotional, social, volitional, physical, and mental.

It is vital that we internalize the vision of shalom, which involves healing and wholeness. God's shalom may make us active participants in God's scheme to help liberate people who are struggling with their captivity to victimhood. It helps heal wounded people's festering wounds. Let the pursuit of wholeness become an imperative in our mission. Let our journey together this biennium be a movement from woundedness toward wholeness for ourselves and all victims of our war-torn nation. Let this vision of wholeness guide our thinking and actions in the 2011-2013 biennium.

Who is this one
who journeys with us?

62nd Session: Jaffna Diocesan Council
of the Church of South India
2013

Welcome and introduction

My dear Sisters and Brothers in Christ.

Welcome to our 62nd Session of the Jaffna Diocesan Council of the Church of South India. I sincerely appreciate your presence in this important event in the life of this great Church. Participation at this Session prepares all of us to view our greater calling and responsibilities in the life and mission of this historic church.

A recapitulation

Most of you will recognize and remember that I presided over the 59th Session in the year 2007, a year after I became the fourth Bishop of the Jaffna Diocese of the Church of South India (JDCSI) on the 21st August 2006. Then I brought to mind the great significance of the Church of South India and the historic legacy our forerunners, the American Missionaries, left for us. I called upon all of us to "Journey Together". After two years, in 2009, I challenged all of us to come together to "Re-build Communities of Hope", taking to heart the challenges of the *kairos* moment in which we were then placed.

Two years later we gathered to discern the will of God for us for the next biennium, 2011-2013. I brought to mind the importance of discerning the different situation prevailing then, to what it was in 2009. I wanted all of to feel the agony of the ones who have undergone untold hardship, tribulation, pain, anxiety and above all, the unprecedented experience of separation, loss and death. The crisis of large displacement affecting many hundreds of thousands of civilians moved our hearts to look for an alternate way of thinking and being. The 'woundedness' of our fellow brethren called for a new paradigm of mission and ministry.

I called for fresh thinking that could help us set aside our own spirit of self–satisfaction, self–boasting and self–justification in what we were trying to do. We brought to mind that abandoning this attitude would help us journey together with a clear vision of the pursuit of wholeness. Hence my charge as Bishop was based on 'Journey toward Wholeness'. We were called to see that our Church's unobtrusive witness should seek only the dignity, healing and common good of those whose lives have been shattered and torn apart. The challenge before us, I affirmed, was first to become 'wounded listeners' in order to become 'wounded healers'.

Such a time like this ....

As we come together once again as sojourners, let us recall what we have done as this historic church in the 2011-13 biennium. I concluded my charge then with the words, 'Let our journey together this biennium be a movement from woundedness toward wholeness. Let this vision of wholeness guide our thinking and actions in this biennium 2011-2013'.

We thank God that our journey in the biennium we have just completed was full of challenges and motivations. We are happy that the JDSCI, through its arm the Centre for Holistic Healing (CHH), has been at the forefront in reaching out to people who eagerly looked up to the church for solace. The church, a community in itself that is often called a community of faith, is also a community that bears witness and lives out its faith in the larger context of the nation. God's imperative is that the church is to model and extend the reign and rule of Christ. It is a kingdom of *shalom*. Peace as *shalom* is more than the absence of war. Formulated negatively, *shalom* includes the absence of alienation, material need, and oppression in society. Formulated positively, *shalom* indicates a state of comprehensive social harmony and material wellbeing in society. We continue to struggle through the question of human solidarity and togetherness. As we continued to be in touch with those who gave their best to re-start their living, we also understand that it is not as easy as we often think. They are the ones who have undergone untold hardships. Major issues of non-acceptance, fear, trauma, post-traumatic stress disorder (PTSD) and above all the continued state of victimhood make us realize the momentous question of reordering human inter-relationships at all levels in justice and peace.

People's yearning for inclusion in the midst of isolation or exclusion is an important issue we are confronted with. Human solidarity is the most urgent question that needs to be answered. We learn through experience that any praxis that is contrary to human solidarity will jeopardize the cause of the victims. The issue of belonging to an authentic community of equals remains the unanswered question of the victims, since it is necessarily connected with the search for authentic selfhood or meaningful existence.

Frustrated, grieving, but not despairing

As we continued with the journey of togetherness and solidarity we also felt that the priorities were fast changing and we often came to a point of discerning the priority of priorities. We felt it a great joy and privilege to have been involved in the mission and ministry of solidarity. However, we were also saddened by desertions of our people, including a few pastors. At times we started to question and reassess our own thinking and actions. We felt so much hurt when the ones who journeyed with us for a common purpose and good then chose different paths. It is true that our spirit of enthusiasm and courage was put to the test at such moments. Often we asked the question 'Et tu, Brute?' ('You too, Brutus?' or 'And you, Brutus?') Whether Julius Caesar said this or not, or whether William Shakespeare was fond of using this line or not is not the matter of our debate! The JDCSI continued to struggle and suffer as some chose to leave us and decided to take another route.

The deaths of two dear, faithful pastors (Presbyters) viz., the Rev. Sivasubramaniam Ariaratnam, fondly called Aria, and the Rev. Sinnathamby Jeyaseelan of the Hill country added much grief to our morale. Difficulties in finding resources and resource people for our mission work often made us weary. For our friend of forty odd years (Aria), I cried (using the words of David), 'I am distressed for you, my brother Aria; greatly beloved were you to me; your love to me was wonderful'. And at the death of the Rev. Jeyaseelan of Ragalle, I wept, 'Blessed are you, Jeyaseelan, for you were faithful in a few things and you now enter into the joy of your Master'. These were the first deaths of those ordained by me. Yes, my heart bleeds at the loss of these dear ones. The only consolation we had was the thought that we still had a faithful and committed group of believers and friends who went out of their way to make us strong in times of weakness. They help us stand firm in times of desperation and need. We joyfully sang Isaac Watt's hymn 'O God our help in ages past; Our hope for years to come; Our shelter from the stormy blast; And our Eternal Home'.

Encouraged to internalize hope and gain vitality

We have been encouraged by the continued support of our mission partners. The UnitingWorld of the Uniting Church in Australia continued to be in partnership. The Sri Lanka Partnership Programme Committee (SLPP) of the Uniting Church in Australia (Melbourne), ably coordinated by a committed group headed by the Rev. John Bottomley, the Uniting Church in Australia Church Council of St George's East St Kilda Uniting Church where the Rev. Mrs. Angela Tampiyappa is the Minster, and the Board of Governance of Creative Ministries Network (CMN) truly deserve our sincere gratitude. We record our thanks for the commitment of JDCSI liaison in Melbourne, Christy Thiagarajah. Pastor Anto Samuel continues to support us in our children's ministry. We are happy with the ongoing support for Harriet Winslow Girls Home, Pandateruppuof Pastors Lucky and Damayanthi Canagasabey of Christian Life Assembly (CLA), Melbourne. We are indebted to the Association Palmyrah – Ecumenical Partnership, Berne, Switzerland and the Swiss League of Catholic Women for their continued support to our 'Solidarity is Strength-Palmyrah Project' and the Centre for Holistic Healing. We are encouraged by the support, concern and care of all who are connected with these two organizations, especially Dr. Damaris Luthi, Dr. Nathalie Payer, Mr. Condradin Mohr and Mr. Udo Prinz, and the Indiana Kentucky Conference of the United Church of Christ, USA. We see a new ray of hope in the reestablishment of our relationship with the Trustees of Jaffna College Funds. We are confident that the Trustees will recognize us as a partner as per the original arrangement and support us in our common mission and ministry.

What shall we say then? – 'We learn through failures'

In the midst of our failures and our experience of desertions and betrayals, we feel more of our need for self-critique and envisioning hope for future. It was a sad day in my own life on September 7th, 2011 when the vehicle I was travelling in met with an 'accident.' I thank God for the miraculous healing God granted me with through God's faithful servants, Dr. Irene Sathiaseelan and Dr.Ariaranee Gnanathasan. Coming to life after two days on life-support equipment and five-days in a coma made me more and more convinced of God's own commitment for God's anointed. Though the question, 'Was it an accident or an incident?' is still not answered and the case file is not closed, yet the fact remains that God is faithful and God's faithfulness never ceases even in the midst human faithlessness.

In my own desperation and agony I prayerfully said three days before Easter, 2013, 'I will rise again on Easter day'. Then I came to understand the divine mystery in the question of theodicy from my good friend and mentor the Rev. John Bottomley, whose words after his own trauma I quote verbatim: '…..But following Paul, I do believe that God has turned events to good through the work of the Holy Spirit. In this faith, I cannot tell you where my healing will lead me. But I am confident that this healing is in God's hand, and is part of his loving purpose. Today, God's Spirit calls us in our weakness. This is sufficient for us to endure and, so, to live'. I thank God for such friends who thoughtfully and prayerfully care for us and the diocese.

And yet It moves

'And yet It moves' – this is what I pick up from the little book, *And Yet It Moves: Dreams and Reality of the Ecumenical Movement*, a masterpiece by Ernst Lange (1927-1974), who is still considered the most influential ecumenist of the 20th century after Dietrich Bonhoeffer. In the midst of unexpected events, disappointments failures and hopelessness we clearly see the hand of God that moves us on.

Many times have I preached and meditated on the Emmaus Story. I last preached on it the Sunday before last at Cheddikulam for the joint confirmations of Adappankulam and Cheddikulam churches. The Emmaus story is a narrative disclosure about how Christ comes to those who have suffered trauma. Why do the disciples not recognize Christ? This is Luke's affirmation about the terrible price of war and trauma, that God may not be visible to us, even when near. Christ may be still unknown to human seeing and hearing. For the disciples, this journey is the gospel's way of measuring the devastating impact of trauma on the participants and witnesses to Christ's violent crucifixion. This is profound: Christ is present with the disciples but unseen, and unseeable due to their trauma. Christ's presence is God's initiative, even when we are too frail and weak to recognize his presence with us.

But Christ does not judge the disciples for their lack of sight or insight. He listens. He teaches. He accepts them. Christ accepts them as they are: hopeless and helpless. And He joins with them in breaking bread. This is the healing grace that allows them to see what had been hidden. What do they see? Luke is not giving testimony for scientific minds of the 21st century; it is not about evidence of a resurrected body. The miracle of resurrection is God in Christ's forgiveness of the disciples' abandonment and betrayal of him in the violent trauma of the cross, (which was a traumatic loss for the disciples) and his acceptance of them in their failures and weakness. While their trauma is terrible to endure, they are not terrible people. The resurrected Christ lifts the veil of the disciples' shame from their eyes. He breaks their shame and self-loathing open in breaking bread with them. So they 'see' with their hearts. This is what renews their mission of forgiveness and opens up for them a large horizon of the common good. Their hearts are renewed in love, and their relationship with Christ is restored, put right, and made just. This is good news for all people.

As we journey together in order to re-build the lives of the shattered ones and help make hope alive, let us remember that the risen Lord joins us, encourages us, and takes us back to the Scripture to be powerful witnesses to the power of resurrection. As we journey together toward wholeness let us not lose sight of the destination. We are called to conversion to God. We are called to remember that our turning to God in conversion is not the first but a second act because our conversion is possible since God has turned to us in love and has become present in Jesus Christ for all humanity. Conversion as human response to the divine turning is an expression of trust in God's faithfulness toward humanity and to the world. We are also called to turn away from the evil and destructive powers in order to turn to the God who turns toward us. It is, in a way, a transformation not only of the mind but also of the entire being. It speaks of a radical change in one's own understanding of the world and oneself. It is a reorientation of consciousness and a conversion of heart. Hence, it implies a new understanding of reality from the perspective of the reign of God.

As we understand the aspect of God joining us to instill hope and to make us bold and courageous, we are also called to discern that the risen Christ demands of us a call to '*metanoia*', which is more than merely accepting forgiveness. It is a call to turn actively towards God's justice and peace. Our identity as Christians cannot be constituted or sustained apart from constant and continued conversion.

Who is this one who journeys with us?

The One who journeys with us is the One who reminds us of the great challenge that lies ahead of us. The One who journeys with us is the One who helps us not to lose sight of the vision of the reign of God. The One who journeys with us is the One who opens our minds to understand the Scripture. The One who journeys with us is the One who continues to break bread with us so that we are reminded of the presence of Christ in the midst of our brokenness and the brokenness of the world.

Friends, let us commit ourselves into the hands of the One who helps us to commit ourselves to *diakonia* in serving human need and in promoting one human family in justice, peace, and the integrity of God's creation, so that the whole of God's creation may experience fullness of life.

As the 10th Assembly of the World Council of Churches (WCC) draws nigh, may we as part of a large and historical church reflect upon its theme, "God of Life, lead us to justice and peace". So let us take to heart that the vision of peace and wholeness the risen Lord provides us with is a vision of peace with justice for all of humanity. It is not one of several options for us. The One who journeys with us stirs our minds and hearts to understand that it is the imperative of our time.

Walking in Christ's Way:
Towards the Reign of God

Special Session: Jaffna Diocesan Council
of the Church of South India
2015

Christ's Way: the way of the cross

Life is often referred to as a pilgrimage or a journey and the People of God are called 'People on the Move' or 'People on a Pilgrimage'. Jesus undertook many journeys during his earthly ministry and they were mostly to and from Jerusalem in John's gospel or towards Jerusalem in the Synoptic gospels. Jesus often called people to follow him, but Mark makes us think about where we are to go following Jesus. For the way (*eis hodos*) Jesus calls people to follow was the way to the cross. On the way Jesus always taught, admonished and cautioned his followers about how they should proceed on the journey. Many wanted to join that pilgrimage and many were called to be part of it. But time and again many who claimed to have clear vision found it difficult to accept Jesus' call and they deviated from the journey. Then others without physical eye-sight were able to follow Jesus on the way once they were healed by him.

The metaphor of journey or sojourn as God's people is a radical one. It is a challenge to the dominant ideologies of our time that yearn for safety, security and placement. For God is understood not as a God who settles and dwells, but as a God who sojourns and moves about. Participation in the life of God for the life of the world calls us to participate in the life of the journeying God. This journey is made known to us in Jesus Christ. The way Mark presents Jesus' journey toward Jerusalem is significant. 'Jesus went on with his disciples to the villages of Caesarea Philippi; and *on the way* he asked his disciples, "Who do people say that I am?"' (Mark 8:27). Jesus did not stop with the response to that question. He continued to ask them, 'But who do you say that I am?' (Mark 8:29). Though Peter answered, 'You are the Messiah', the disciples did not truly understand what kind of Messiah he was. On the contrary, they were arguing on the way as to who would be the greatest amongst them. Hence Jesus taught them on discipleship. The same pattern continued as Jesus journeyed beyond Caesarea Philippi towards Jerusalem. This may portray the inability of the disciples to comprehend the Messiahship of Jesus as they were on the way with him. But the blind man Bartimaeus was able to understand Jesus and followed him on the way. With this Mark takes the reader into the Jerusalem narrative.

The way of the kingdom: promise and warnings

It is more than thirty years ago since the Commission for World Mission and Evangelism (CWME) organized a World Conference in Melbourne, Australia on the theme 'Thy Kingdom Come'. Bishopamma had the privilege to attend their very next conference held in San Antonio, Texas, USA in 1989 and it is pertinent that its theme of 'Thy Will Be Done' was also chosen from the Lord's Prayer. However, it is interesting to note that while Matthew and Luke both give an account of the Lord's Prayer, Luke omits the supplication 'thy will be done' but retains 'thy kingdom come'. With this supplication one gets into the very heart of the Lord's Prayer, which states the ultimate intention of Jesus. The proclamation of the Kingdom of God constitutes the core of Jesus' message and the primary motives of his activities.

Jesus, according to Mark's Gospel, began his ministry by saying, 'The time (*kairos*) is fulfilled, and the Kingdom of God has come near; repent, and believe in the good news' (1$^{:15}$). To avoid speaking of God directly, Matthew prefers the phrase 'Kingdom of Heaven'. When the disciples were sent for mission, he focused their message in the same words, 'The Kingdom of Heaven is at hand' (Matt. 10$^{:17}$ cf. Luke 10$^{:9}$). Also, according to Matthew, with Jesus' parable being the main method of his teaching, the parables begin with the words, 'The Kingdom (of Heaven) is like …' (Matt.13$^{:24,31,33,44,45,47}$). While the phrase 'Kingdom of God' occurs thirteen times in Mark, 'Kingdom of Heaven' occurs thirty-six times in Matthew and eighteen times in Luke. The Synoptic gospels emphasis on the 'Kingdom' or 'Kingdom of God' reveals this is a memorable and central aspect in Jesus' ministry. Indeed, the crux of the gospel message revolves around this one important theme, 'Kingdom of God'. Jesus called people to immediate action because the Kingdom of God has already broken in. People cannot but respond to this message. In order to comprehend the meaning of this, one should begin at a distance and dig deeply. Only then will its radical nature and novelty be appreciated.

It is said that the human being is not so much a *being* as a *becoming*. Only human beings dream in their sleeping and waking hours of new worlds where interpersonal relationships will be always more egalitarian. Only humans envision a new heaven and a new earth. Only humans dream of utopias. Anthropologists say that human beings are inhabited by a '*hope principle*'. All human cultures have their utopias. In other words, they constitute the womb of all hope. The Judeo-Christian tradition, beginning in the Hebrew Scriptures, speaks of the transfiguration wrought by God for God's people in the present world in all its relationships. The eighth century prophet Isaiah speaks about the reconciliation of nature, when 'the wolf shall live with the sheep… the lion shall eat straw like cattle, the infant shall play over the hole of the cobra, and … they shall not hurt or destroy in all my holy mountain' (Isaiah 11:6-9). Jeremiah spoke of God creating a new covenant written on human hearts (Jeremiah 31:33).

Our tradition is steadfast in this promised hope. Prophets have always appeared, not allowing hope to die: one day God is going to intervene and restore everything to its original goodness and raise everything to a fullness never dreamed of in the past. The Old Testament points to it again and again. When Moses led the liberation of the Israelites from Egyptian slavery, their testimony is that 'The Lord shall reign forever and ever!' (Ex. 15:18) From the darkness of Israel's exile, their prophets speak of God's saving power. Isaiah declares, 'I am Yahweh: those who wait for me shall not be put to shame' (Isaiah 49:23), while Jeremiah says, 'I am going to teach them my power and my might, and they shall know that my name is the Lord' (Jeremiah 16:21). These are promises of God's faithfulness and fidelity to the covenant with God's people that nurture hope in situations of conflict. The overall meaning is clear: God is not indifferent to the cry that rises to heaven. God is here and will make God's reign manifest.

Another major thrust in the Old Testament era was the expectation that the lordship of God would become manifest in the lordship of the king of Israel (2 Sam. 7:12-16). Therefore the notion of kingship in Israel was highly anticipated. It held the great expectation that the king would bring justice to the poor and be an instrument of God in restoring the rights of widows, and defending orphans. The king was to be one who would liberate the world from its unjust principles. However, within a short time the corruption of power became evident in the very kings who were supposed to represent God, taking the title "Son of God" (cf. Ps. 2:7; 2 Sam. 7:14). The fears expressed earlier through the prophet Samuel apparently came true.

The regulated temple worship, with its priestly orders, sacrifices, and prescriptions for holiness was thought to be the means by which God would reign from the temple, where God's people would encounter God as though face to face (see Ezekiel 40-43). But the prophets vehemently condemned and denounced any illusions of a worship that excluded conversion, fellowship, and mercy (Amos 5:21-24). The worship that God wants is justice and liberation of the oppressed (Isaiah 1:17). The fast God chooses or wills, as recorded in Isaiah 58:1-12 is the expression of God's hospitality to the world at large. The living God is an ethical God who commands worship that despises iniquity and rejoices with the just.

Another group put its hope in a universal reconciliation in an apocalyptic sense. They sought a secret wisdom, one that was accessible only to the initiated. This community believed their special wisdom allowed them to interpret the signs of the times. They anticipated a cosmic revolution and the emergence of a new heaven and a new earth. This event would come suddenly and would invert every relationship: the unhappy would become happy and the happy unhappy, the poor would become rich and the rich poor, outcasts would be honored and the honored despised. This seems like the realization of Mary's song— the Magnificat. Along with this sudden transformation would come the end of this world and the inauguration of a new heaven and a new earth. The

New Testament visionary John spoke about a time when people would no longer feel hunger or thirst (Revelation 7:16). Hence, the Messianic times are presented as days when all of these dreams of a new heaven and a new earth finally come true.

Whereas the apocalyptics expected the kingdom to come of its own accord, the Zealots, another group of enthusiasts, felt that they should accelerate the coming of the kingdom by the use of violence. Others, such as the deeply pious Pharisees, thought that by strict observance of the divine law, even to the extent of separating themselves from those not following the law, they would accelerate the coming of this universal transformation.

God's coming kingdom: the in-breaking reality of God's solidarity with the poor

But all this was in vain. And the supplication that arose to God was: Thy kingdom come! May the fullness of time come! It is against this background of hope and anxiety that the voice of Jesus of Nazareth echoed in Galilee to the rural and oppressed peasants and others: 'The time is fulfilled; the Kingdom of God has come near; repent, and believe in the good news' (Mark 1:15). This is no mere promise, like that of all the prophets before him: the kingdom will come! Instead, Jesus says: the kingdom is already at hand.

To walk in Christ's way is to participate and announce the constant in-breaking of God's rule into all of life. 'The time is near: repent and believe in the gospel" (Mark 1:15). Despite all the problems and ambiguities, this is a life into which God's rule (Kingdom) has been released. We are called to discern the signs of the kingdom, and Jesus instructs his followers about the signs of the kingdom. It is healing of lives, driving out the forces that enslave people, and teaching a new way of being and acting.

The unmistakable signs that the kingdom is already in effect are that 'the blind recover their sight, the lame walk, lepers are made clean, the deaf hear, the dead are raised to life, and the poor are hearing the good news' (Luke 7:22). Jesus accomplished all this and then sent word of it to John the Baptist (Luke 7:18-23). The prophet Isaiah first announced these signs (Isaiah 61:1-2), and Jesus authoritatively declared these same signs were being manifested in his ministry: 'Today in your very hearing this text has come true' (Luke 4:21). Jesus announces that the Kingdom of God is the reign of God's solidarity with the poor and oppressed. To follow Jesus is to go to the poor, the marginalized, and the oppressed in society with the good news that they are the children of God. Albert Nolan said, 'The option for the poor is not a choice about the recipients of the gospel message, to whom we must preach the gospel; it is a matter of what gospel we preach to anyone at all. It is concerned with the gospel message itself!'

The coming of the Kingdom of God is the message of hope and joy proclaimed by Jesus. Here, 'kingdom' does not refer to a territory but to the divine power and authority that now is in this world, transforming the old into new, the unjust into just, and sickness into health. Jesus meant something dynamic when speaking of God's coming kingdom. He used parables to explain its meaning. It is like a treasure hidden in a field; whoever comes upon it sells everything in order to buy the field (Matt. 13:44). It is like a precious pearl whose acquisition involves sacrificing everything (Matt. 13:45). It is like a tiny seed that grows and becomes so large that the birds build their nests in it (Matt. 13:31; Mark 4:26-32). It is a force that transforms everything (Matt. 13:33).

Jesus summarized the Ten Commandments with the double commandment to love God and one's neighbor. First, he insisted that one cannot love God without loving one's neighbor, and then, he removed all limits to who my neighbor is. In the Jewish worldview 'neighbor' tended to mean 'fellow-Jew.' Jesus expanded neighbor to mean all people, even one's own enemies. Thus he radicalized the law of the kingdom by making it clearer that it is not love of God and love of neighbor, but love of God by love of neighbor, with no limits to who is the neighbor.

Accepting God's coming kingdom and living out God's love

From Jesus' whole ministry it is absolutely clear that the only fitting response to the coming of the kingdom is a *metanoia*, a change of heart. His announcement of the kingdom is a call to live according to the will of God. Since God wills to love all people, the will of God necessarily requires one's conversion to his/her neighbor. In Greek language the word 'repent' had two predominant meanings. The primary meaning was 'to change one's mind,' and from this comes the secondary meaning, 'to regret, or to feel remorse'. But the word used by Jesus would have called for more than a change of mind and an expression of regret or remorse. The distinctively Jewish notion of repentance was much more radical. The nearest Hebrew equivalent had the meaning 'turn around'. It involved turning around, a radical alteration of the course and direction of one's life, its motivations and objectives.

Schillebeeckx calls this the praxis of the kingdom of God, a *metanoia* that causes us to live out its coming faithfully in a consistent way of living. What Jesus called for was conversion, for a turning round of heart and will and life, as well as a change of mind. He called for a conversion that was the end of self-serving and self-justification, the recognition of the delusion that material possessions could meet our human need for identity and purpose, and the realization of where a person's true worth and long term good lies. Jesus' proclamation of the kingdom is a proclamation of how human life ought to be lived. As the kingdom is a manifestation of God's love for humanity, human beings manifest the kingdom by loving God and/through their neighbor. When Jesus calls people to fellowship with him, he calls them to service in the world. Gustaf Aulen says in *Jesus in Contemporary Historical Research*, 'To live in the fellowship of Jesus is to be called as his fellow worker in the service of man (sic).' Members of the kingdom are not objects acted upon by God's activity, but subjects called to respond to God's Kingdom by living their lives in partnership for each other. Jesus preached the kingdom as a symbol of both hope and command. It is hope because it is the promise and assurance of God's saving activity that will finally bring all things within God's sovereign will. Since God's activity calls for human activity in response, it is also a command. It is a call to obey God's will that in turn demands conversion to the neighbor whom God wills humans to love.

The kingdom as symbol of hope and command leads to a related question concerning Jesus' preaching of the kingdom. If the kingdom is coming to its fullness by the grace and power of God, what then is the role of our human response in its ongoing coming? Nowhere is it recorded that Jesus ever said, 'Go and build the Kingdom. But he did say that we are to seek it first (Matt. $6^{:33}$) and to be like good soil which brings forth much fruit (Matt.$13^{:4-23}$); also that the kingdom is like an invaluable treasure or a pearl of great price to be sought above all things (Matt. $13^{:44-46}$). In other words, although Jesus proclaimed the kingdom as a

---

[1] G. Aulen, *Jesus in Contemporary Historical Research*. Trans. I. H. Hjelm. Philadelphia: Fortress Press, 1976, p.144.

gift coming by the grace and power of God, he also demanded of its members an active response according to the values of the kingdom within time and history.

God's kingdom as liberation for the poor and oppressed

Jesus Christ, when he began his ministry, entered into the synagogue of Nazareth and read the words of the prophet Isaiah to let the hearers know the purpose of his coming into the world:

"The Spirit of the Lord is upon me,

because he has anointed me

to bring good news to the poor.

He has sent me to proclaim release to the captives

And recovery of sight to the blind,

To let the oppressed, go free, to proclaim the year of the Lord's favor."

(Luke 4:18-19)

Jesus' message was that all that could destroy life should be overcome. Note that while the Synoptic Gospels emphasize the Kingdom of God, the Fourth Gospel speaks about Life. In other words the values of the kingdom are summed up by the one word LIFE in the Fourth Gospel. Therefore, when these values are threatened, life itself is threatened. If one says that the will of God for Jesus was to establish God's Kingdom, then the proclamation of God's Kingdom was in fact announcing the liberation of God's creation from every form of enslavement that denies life!

For Boff, the process of liberation as Christ's salvation expresses a people's utopian longing for liberation from all that alienates them: pain, hunger, injustice, and death. Similarly Gustavo Gutierrez has succinctly stated that in the perspective of the Kingdom the core of liberation is to participate in the struggle for the liberation of those oppressed by others. The love of God towards humanity is so great that it consists of total liberation of humanity. Therefore, Paul says, 'Neither death, nor life, nor angels, nor rulers, nor things present, nor things to come, nor powers, nor height, nor depth, nor anything else in all creation will be able to separate us from the love of God in Christ Jesus' (Romans 8:38-39). Therefore, humanity can grasp this love of God through God's concern for what God has created and is still willing to recreate. God identifies Godself with humanity's poor. Christians are called forth to participate in this supreme act of God's love.

The Roman Catholic Bishops who first met in Medelin in the year 1968 and deliberated on the preferential option for the poor, ratified it after seven years in Puebla, saying in unison 'The love of God for us today must become first and foremost a labor of justice on behalf of the oppressed, an effort of liberation for those who are most in need of it'. Love of God and love of neighbor, especially love of the poor cannot be separated. The Parable of the Last Judgment in Matthew 25 summarizes the very essence of this Gospel message. Christ is to be found in the hungry, the thirsty and the naked. The parable talks about the hidden brotherhood of Christ. The important point here is that God's judgment is given not on the basis of what people had done but mainly on the basis of what they had left undone! At the same time one should also understand God's identification with the marginalized not just as a question of charity but of justice! In this connection what the prophet Jeremiah uttered is important: 'He judged the cause of the poor and needy; then it was well. Is not this to know me? Says the Lord' (Jer.22:16).

The Church is the sacrament of God's power and presence here on earth in today's world, which is divided sharply along the lines of wealth and affluence on the one hand, and poverty and deprivation on the other. The question is 'how can the Church retain its sacramentality?' The signs of this sacramentality are signs related to the poor! Hence, the announcement of the in-breaking of the reign of God is, in reality, confrontation with all those powers that would militate against such an announcement!

Jose Miranda in his *Marx and the Bible – A Critique of the Philosophy of Oppression* (Maryknoll, Orbis, 1980) says, 'One cannot claim to know Yahweh except by doing justice. To know Yahweh is to achieve justice for the poor'. Let me conclude with what this means for our Diocese today. If we are to be the bearer of the Kingdom, then the struggle for liberation is not only one of political demands, but is fundamentally about the demands of the faith. It is time for us to be at work for God's current newness. It is the opportune moment to think with the risk-taking spirit of our forebears. It is truly the *kairos* context to be the womb for birthing a new wonder in the world. Let us go out, not in anxiety and anguish but in joy and in peace. Let us blaze a trail with Christ's footprints that shows we are clearly out from tired old stuff, from fears that divide us, from sins unforgiven, and from quarrels unresolved in order to walk in Christ's way into God's new and demanding mission.

Speaking the Truth in Love
63rd Session: Jaffna Diocesan Council of the Church of South India
2015

Welcome & introduction

My dear Sisters and Brothers in Christ,

Welcome to our 63rd Session of the Jaffna Diocesan Council of the Church of South India. I sincerely appreciate your presence in this important event in the life of this great Church. I give a special welcome to our Ecumenical friends who are here. Thank you for honoring our invitation. This is an important Session as we recognize the presence of our Sinhalese brethren who are joining us from down South – Matara, Hambantota, Neluwa, Baddegama, Galle and Panadura; from the North-West – Kurunegala, Kuliyapitiya, Mawathegama and Kegalle. What a joy it is for all of us when we gather from North and South, West and East, and from the Central Hills to recollect the words of our Lord Jesus Christ, for we are all a part of this great legacy and experience the joy of our God that God's house is filled with all! As you are well aware, participation at this Session prepares all of us to view our greater calling and responsibilities in the life and mission of this historic church.

A recapitulation

When I look back, what do I see? Shall I say that I called all of us to 'journey together' in the very first Council I addressed as Bishop? Or, may I say that we discussed together the ways to 're-build hope' in 2009 in the midst of all kinds adverse situations? Maybe we will not forget the determination we had when we gathered for the 61st Session in 2011 to 'journey toward wholeness' amidst chaos, destruction, loss of hope and shattered lives! Truly, as we gathered once again in 2013 we struggled together to discern and take to heart the 'One who journeys with us'!

Now when we respond to the call to gather again for the 63rd Session, what do we say? The political situation in our country is somewhat better than when we were here last. Most of us desired for a change and looked forward to that. Thank God, we begin to experience a change, a change for the better! However, many burning questions still come over and again in our hearts. Perhaps we, as humans, are often overcome by a spirit of pessimism instead of optimism. However we are encouraged with the words of Paul, 'But we have this treasure in clay jars, so that it may be made clear that this extraordinary power belongs to God and does not come from us. We are afflicted in every way, but not crushed; perplexed, but not driven to despair; persecuted, but not forsaken; struck down, but not destroyed; always carrying in the body the death of Jesus, so that the life of Jesus may also be made visible in our bodies. For while we live, we are always being given up to death for Jesus' sake, so that the life of Jesus may be made visible in our mortal flesh. So death is at work in us, but life in you' (2 Cor. 4:7-12, NRSV).

The task ahead of us

Hence, we need to take to heart that our experience is that of a victor despite our struggles as victims. Discerning aright the One who has called us continues to journey with us to give us strength to go ahead with determination to be effective servants in the vineyard of God. Mahatma Gandhi is often quoted as rightly saying, '*When I despair, I remember that all through history the way of truth and love have always won. There have been tyrants and murderers, and for a time, they can seem invincible, but in the end, they always fall. Think of it—always*'. *We are overwhelmed by the power that gives us victory because we have this power that belongs to God and not to us, and it is contained in earthen jars so that even if the jar is wasted away, the power is in union with the One who ultimately triumphs.*

I still remember the day when I went to submit my evidence before the President's Truth and Reconciliation Commission (LLRC) in Colombo. Some of you present here were there when I testified. I emphasized three major components viz., truth-telling, pursuit for justice and healing the wounds, which were necessary for a peaceful co-existence and harmonious living.

In Sri Lanka, while offering divergent accounts of the conduct of Sri Lanka's armed forces during the last stages of the war, reports by the UN Secretary General's Panel of Experts and the domestic Lessons Learnt and Reconciliation Commission (LLRC) both appeared to agree on critical aspects of transitional justice, such as the importance of ensuring truth, justice and reparations in respect of the past. In any justice system, truth is non-negotiable and precedes restitution. Good governance does not mean clinging to power at the expense of truth and justice. We need to know that failure to honor demands for transitional justice for minorities is not compatible with the moral integrity of good governance, nor could it be sustainable in the long term.

Truth-telling: a Biblical understanding

We are to know God, to know the truth of God. 'This is eternal life, that they may know you, the only true God, and Jesus Christ whom you have sent' (Jn. 17:3). Jesus came to bear witness to the truth (cf. Jn. 18:37) and presented himself as 'the way, and the truth, and the life' (Jn. 14:6). This truth is a gift which comes down from 'the Father of lights' (James 1:17). God the Father initiated this enlightenment (cf. Gal 4:4-7), and he himself will consummate it (cf. Rev. 21:5-7). The Holy Spirit is both the Paraclete, consoling the faithful, and the 'Spirit of truth' (Jn. 14:16 17) who inspires and illuminates the truth and guides the faithful 'into all the truth' (Jn. 16:13). The final revelation of the plenitude of God's truth will be the ultimate fulfillment of humanity and of creation (cf. 1Cor 15:28).

The truth of God, accepted in faith, encounters human reason. Created in the image and likeness of God (Gen. 1:26-27), the human person is capable, by the light of reason, to penetrate beyond appearances to the deep-down truth of things and open up thereby to universal reality. The common reference to truth, which is objective and universal, makes authentic dialogue possible between human persons.

Virtually everyone knows that the people of God are supposed to tell the truth. We remember how Jesus described himself as 'the way and the truth and the life' (John 14:6), and we understand that truth is the way of life God calls us to. Honesty and telling the truth are highly valued by God and are considered an integral part of a life of integrity and faithfulness to him. The Mosaic Law commands that God's people do not lie or deceive each other (Leviticus 19:11) or give false testimony about another (Exodus 20:16). The Psalmist describes the person whose walk is blameless and righteous as speaking the truth from the heart (Psalm 15:2). The New Testament echoes this when it connects honesty and truthfulness with the believer's new life in Christ (Colossians 3:9). One of the first manifestations of the believer putting off the old self and putting on the new self in Christ is a commitment to honesty (Ephesians 4:24-25). The virtue of honesty is grounded ultimately in the character of God—that is, we are to be truthful because God is truthful. The Bible informs us that God never lies (Titus 1:2), and both Jesus and the Holy Spirit are referred to as *the truth* (John 14:6, 16:13; 1 John 5:6). Similarly, God's word is called the truth (Psalm 119:142, John 17:17). Truth-telling is a moral principle to be followed because God is truthful, and we are called to emulate his character.

The basic attitude of human faith is 'speaking the truth in love, we must grow up in every way into him who is the head, into Christ' (Ephesians 4:15). 'For we cannot do anything against the truth, but only for the truth' (2 Corinthians 13:8). Truth-telling treats people with dignity. To tell someone the truth is a measure of respect that is missing when someone is lied to.

The centrality of speaking the truth in love

Paul, when writing his Letter to the People of God in Ephesus, emphasizes the centrality of speaking the truth in love. Verses 4:25-5:5 are clearly marked as a unit because Paul delivers six commands/instructions.

(1)   Do not use falsehood

         but speak truth   4:25

(2)   Do use anger but do not sin   4:26-27

(3)	Do not steal but work to	
	give to the needy	4:28

(4)	Do not use corrupt words	
	but edify	4:29-30

(5)	Do not have a mean spirit	
	but be kind	4:31-32
	love one another	5:1-2

(6)	No impure actions/words	
	or greed	5:3-5

If there is any way to summarize in just a few words the instructions for behavior and conduct in the community of the new creation, it is 'speaking the truth in love'. This central notion of speaking the truth in love was expressed in 4:15 by the Greek verb *alētheuō* whereas here in 4:25 the verb 'speak' plus the noun 'truth' is used as its object. For the former word, *alētheuō*, Bauer's lexicon gives the meaning 'be truthful, speak the truth'. Indeed, Greek verbs ending in *-euō* have the meaning 'to act in a certain capacity or role.'[1] The verb *alētheuō*, then, means 'to *act* truthfully'. Since this kind of action frequently involves our speech, a common meaning is 'to speak truthfully. While the first of the six commands given by Paul is specifically about speaking, and indeed four or five of the six instructions either may or necessarily involve speech, 'acting or being truthful' does sum up all of them. And this acting or being truthful must be expressed in love, as the paragraph in 5:1-2 inserted between the fifth and sixth command indicates. This paragraph is a summary of all the commands and instructions.

---

[1] J. H. Moulton and W. F. Howard, *A Grammar of New Testament Greek* vol. 2, *Accidence and Word-Formation*; Edinburgh: T. & T. Clark, 1929, 398-400.

First, it condenses everything to one command or instruction. Second, it explains why this behavior, this conduct, this lifestyle, is required of us: our actions and our words come from who we are. Ephesians 5$^{:1-2}$ is directly related to 4$^{:24}$ where we see that we have become part of the new creation in which the divine image is restored. The conduct of the new humanity must reflect the character and conduct of God himself. Third, since the cross is at the heart of who God is, it is also at the heart of who we are as his children. We can, therefore, define love as a *covenant commitment* to the other person demonstrated in actions that seek the wellbeing of the other person.

It is clear that the expression 'speaking the truth in love' is central to the message and structure of this Ephesian text as a whole. Certain questions may be raised in order to understand the text. Is it simply being honest and telling the truth, yet at the same time, doing it in a kindly way? Is this the way for the church to grow and mature until it measures up to Christ himself? Furthermore, if the expression 'speaking the truth in love' summarizes living up to the standards of the new humanity, what beyond mere obedience to the commands of Christ is the motivation for living this way?

A careful reader will understand that the command to speak the truth is a citation from the Old Testament. Paul is directly quoting Zechariah 8$^{:16}$, which is just the tip of the iceberg! We may know that the prophet Zechariah wrote to the Jewish people who were returning to their homeland after years of exile in Babylon. It may be observed that the Book begins with a call to repent and a promise that if the people turn away from their sins and return to the Lord, the Lord will return to them (Zech. 1$^{:3}$). Through a series of apocalyptic night visions (chapters 1-6) the prophet announces a return from exile far greater than just leaving Babylon and returning to Jerusalem. It will be a totally different experience for them. Their sins will be forgiven, the broken covenant will be renewed, the city of God will be restored, the temple will be rebuilt, and God the Lord will return to live once more in the midst of God's people as King!

The seventh and eighth chapters speak about the shift of experience from fasting to feasting. When one reads this chiastically,[1] it is noteworthy that at the centre of the chiasm ($8^{:8b}$) one finds the covenant formula, 'They will be my people and I will be their God in faithfulness and righteousness'. A few lines earlier, in $8^{:3}$, we read, 'I will return to Zion and I will settle in the midst of Jerusalem. And Jerusalem will be called the City of Truth and the mountain of the Lord of Heaven's Armies will be called the Holy Mountain'. Hence, when the covenant is renewed, Jerusalem is called the City of Truth. This is exactly the spirit of the Pauline passage (Eph. $4{:}1\text{-}6^{:20}$). That is, Paul describes the new covenant and shows that speaking the truth results in the covenant community life. Zechariah $8^{:16}$ tells what it means for Jerusalem to regain its title as the City of Truth. 'But this is what you must do: Tell the truth to each other. Render verdict in your courts that are just and that lead to peace'. Hence one may clearly see that 'truth' in Zechariah operates in the context of social justice within the community!

Discovering the meaning of speaking the truth in Ephesians, Paul exhorts the church to adopt and use Yahweh's own armor for warfare, he draws specifically from Isa. $11^{:4\text{-}5}$ and $59^{:17}$. The

---

[2] A chiasm (also called a chiasmus) is a literary device in which a sequence of ideas is presented and then repeated *in reverse order*. The result is a "mirror" effect as the ideas are "reflected" back in a passage. Each idea is connected to its "reflection" by a repeated word, often in a related form. https://www.gotquestions.org/chiasm-chiastic.html (accessed 6/1/2020).

first passage brings to a climax the promise of a coming scion of David, indeed a new David, whose rule will be characterized by social justice. Isaiah 11[:3b-5] states, 'He will not judge by what he sees with his eyes, or decide by what he hears with his ears; but with righteousness he will judge the needy, with justice he will give decisions for the poor of the earth. He will strike the earth with the rod of his mouth; with the breath of his lips he will slay the wicked. Righteousness will be his belt and faithfulness the sash around his waist '(NIV). Paul's belt of truth comes from the last part of verse 5: 'faithfulness (will be) the sash around his waist'. The word 'faithfulness' translates *'emûnâ* and is related to *'emeth*, the usual word for truth. Both are derived from a root meaning to be firm or faithful. Verse 4 combines justice and righteousness to communicate the idea of social justice. Another Isaianic text Paul alludes to is chapter 59 that contains three occurrences of the broken word-pair 'justice-righteousness'. Another word-pair that is seen is 'loving kindness and truth. (Hebrew: *hesed* and *'emeth*).

An in-depth study of the Scripture reveals to us that 'faithful love and social justice' are found in the creation story (humans are created as the divine image). At the heart of the divine image is a right relationship to God on the one hand and a right relationship to the world on the other. It is social justice or loving kindness and truth that is, being truthful in love.

The challenge to the churches

With this background we need to discern the challenge that is before us as churches going forward. It is the task of the whole people of God, to listen to and distinguish the many voices of our times and to interpret them in the light of the divine Word, in order that the revealed truth may be more deeply penetrated, better understood, and more suitably presented. The people of

God believe that we are led by the Spirit of the Lord who fills the whole world. What is happening in the world at large, good or bad, can never be a matter of indifference to the Church. We must be aware of and understand the aspirations, the yearnings, and the often dramatic features of the world in which we live. At all times the Church carries the responsibility of reading the signs of the times (*signa temporum perscrutandi*) and interpreting them in the light of the Gospel, if it is to carry out its task.

The question that is before us is this. A country that is profoundly broken by civil conflict, by economic exclusion, by disease, and by a failure to acknowledge the human dignity of the other is a way of describing our recent experience of the brokenness of societies, and individuals within societies. If reconciliation and healing figure strongly in understanding how to respond to such a world, can they be seen as constituting a new paradigm of mission, that is, a paradigm of presenting the good news of what God is doing in Jesus Christ for our world today? The churches are called to become channels of reconciliation, peace and harmony. Therefore, it is a matter of truth-telling self-awareness or self-critique in order to learn from our lapses and failures so that we become strong in our determination.

Truth-telling is an act where the community validates individual memory. The basis for healing the past is truth-telling. Truth-telling consists first of all in speaking aloud those things kept secret or hidden during the conflict. It is only as things can be spoken aloud in a safe environment that the lessons of the past can be truthfully learned. Truth implies sincerity as well as factuality or reality. The literal meaning of the Greek word for truth ἀλήθεια is, 'the state of not being hidden; the state of being evident'. People were often not allowed to speak of the atrocities which they had witnessed in totalitarian regimes or the bitter divisions of civil war. One could not raise the question of what had happened to loved ones taken away by the police or the armed forces. Speaking the truth breaks through the wall of silence imposed upon a society. Truth-telling necessarily counters the falsehoods and lies perpetrated by the wrongdoers to legitimate their violent wrongdoing. It is a matter of trying to establish just what did happen and why it happened. Hence it is an essential ingredient for the new society. The process of establishing the truth provides a pattern of truthfulness and honesty on which any new political order must be built.

Truth-telling (speaking the truth) is the starting point in any attempt of the community that yearns for human dignity and meaningful existence. It provides a forum for the establishment of justice that paves the way for the affirmation of the divine image in humans. Talking about speaking the truth is not enough. It may give satisfaction to the one who raises their voice. It seldom helps the people against whom truth is hidden. Hence we need to explore a new way to speak the truth. That way, as Paul painstakingly brings forth, is speaking the truth in love. It is not something Paul invented. It is something he clearly modeled for his theology in action. It is the paradigm he internalized through an experience on his journey to Damascus. It is a call to new perspectives.

In the story of the Gerasene demoniac (Mark 5$^{:1-20}$), we read that Jesus entered the scene to bring peace to the man, reinstating his humanity. The movement from woundedness to wholeness is completed by the final action of Jesus: 'Go home to your family and tell them how much the Lord has done for you, and how he has had mercy on you' (verse 19). The wounded community always longs for healing and wholeness. While truth-telling is the starting point it is not the destination. The truth must be said in love. That love demands that we become channels to give them dignity, from their state of abandonment to the state of blessing. There's a difference between loving people and accepting who they are, and how they are, and still understanding that God desires God's people to be whole.

I was fascinated to read Professor Miroslav Volf's book, *Exclusion and Embrace: A Theological Exploration of Identity, Otherness, and Reconciliation* (Abingdon Press. Nashville.1996). Professor Volf was born in Osijek, Croatia. He is a theologian from the former Yugoslavia, which is a country that has seen much conflict over the years and is the founding Director of the Yale Center for Faith and Culture. *His book, Free of Charge: Giving and Forgiving in a Culture Stripped of Grace* (2006), was the Archbishop of Canterbury's Lenten book for 2006. In *Exclusion and Embrace*, we get an in-depth look at a theology of reconciliation. A key theological resource for Volf is found in the work of his doctoral mentor, Jurgen Moltmann. In the following quotation, Moltmann's influence comes through: 'Hanging on the cross, Jesus provided the ultimate example of his command to replace the principle of retaliation (an eye for an eye and a tooth for a tooth) with the principle of nonresistance (if anyone strikes you on the right cheek, turn the other also) (Matthew $5^{:38\text{-}42}$). By suffering violence as an innocent victim, he took upon himself the aggression of the persecutors. He broke the vicious cycle of violence by absorbing it, taking it upon himself. He refused to be sucked into the automatism of revenge.'[3]

What I am trying to assert is the need for a new language that demonstrates our faith. We should not be accused for not getting there in terms of seeing, performing, or experiencing healings. Reconciliation and healing constitute a paradigm for mission.

---

[3] Conversations with Miroslav Volf on Exclusion and Embrace', The Conrad Grebel Review, Special Issue: Miroslav Volf, 18, no. 3 (2000), 291-292.

Concepts of truth-telling and the pursuit of justice are reorganized not just to address wrongdoing and justice in general, but as ways of allowing truth and justice to heal the memories of the past and work toward a different kind of future. Let the language of love, a language we learn from our Lord Jesus Christ and a language internalized by Paul also become our language for today.

I was invited to present a paper at a consultation jointly organized by the Christian Institute for the Study of Religion and Society (CISRS) and the Church of South India Synod. Maybe I end this charge by quoting what I said there as a conclusion, 'God's grace is the divine origin of *diakonia*. God demonstrated it in the act of God making space within Godself to accommodate the creation. God reiterated God's commitment by sending God's Son, Jesus to be the agent of reconciliation and shalom-making by way of *diakonia*. Jesus came proclaiming the reign of God and showed it by acts of compassion with the aim of bringing unity to all things. He also demonstrated that humility is the other side of *diakonia*. Jesus' ministry was evident through the acts of healing being the central mark of his *diakonia* that clearly depicts his true identity as Messiah.

Paul, having followed in the footsteps of Jesus and having understood the inseparable connection between creation and incarnation on the one hand and *kenosis* on the other, brought a message of newness, new life, new creation and new community to convey a new ecclesiology based on *diakonia* as a necessary form of existence and social configuration that constitutes the Church.'

Speaking the truth in love is nothing less than becoming participants in the sacrificial ministry of our Lord for the sake of our world that longs for liberation from its state of victimhood.

Ambassadors for Christ's Ministry of Reconciliation

64th Session: Jaffna Diocesan Council of the Church of South India
2016

2 Corinthians 5:18-20

At the beginning of our 63rd Session of the Jaffna Diocesan Council of the Church of South India, I gave a special welcome to our Sinhalese brethren. This welcome recognized a new movement in the life of JDCSI. At this Council meeting, Paul's call for us to be ambassadors for Christ's ministry of reconciliation now calls us to understand what the presence of our Sinhala brethren means for all of us.

Today, Paul may open our eyes to see that as we are all in Christ we are therefore a new creation (2 Cor. $5^{:17}$). Today, JDCSI is a new creation. Today as we begin the 64th Session of JDCSI, I welcome you to participate in the life of a national church. I do not welcome you as a Tamil bishop leading a Tamil church. Nor do I welcome our Sinhala brethren to be assimilated into what was an historic Tamil church. No. As Paul says, 'the old things have passed away, behold new things have come to be' (5:17). By God's reconciling grace we are a new reality, and our calling is to embody what has been given to us by God. We are called to be Christ's ambassadors entrusted with the message of reconciliation.

So I welcome you as a Church of South India (CSI) bishop of a national church called to serve Christ's ministry of reconciliation in our post-war Sri Lankan nation. Again, Paul helps us to understand what it means for all of us that we are in Christ a new creation.

First, and significantly, Paul says 'the old things have gone'. The history we have told about our missionary forebears is no longer inclusive of our new state of being. We are called to tell a new story about how we became a new creation that includes both Singhalese and Tamil communities. The old story of how JDCSI became a Tamil church is a story of the transgressions of 19th century American and British missionaries who accommodated themselves to colonial powers that divided the country up for their missions according to political patronage and political expediency. Today, we are a new creation because 'God was in Christ reconciling Godself to the world and has not counted the world's transgressions against them' (5:19).

This new story will begin when our thanks for those who brought the gospel to our country also gives voice to our repentance for their exclusivism that set Christianity against Buddhism and Hinduism, bequeathing our nation with forms of Hindu and Buddhist exclusivism that today mirror the same spirit of destructive exclusivism to others that was an integral part of these missionaries evangelical zeal. Paul gives us the guide for our new story and new reality: 'We put no obstacles in anybody's way, so that nobody will say abusive things about our ministry' (6:3). From today, let our commitment to evangelism make Paul's standard for our relationships with our Hindu and Buddhist neighbors be our standard for all JDCSI pastors and congregations.

This new story will begin when our thanks for those who brought the gospel also gives voice to our repentance for the history of education at Batticotta Seminary and later at Jaffna College that rewarded Christian graduates with a path to privilege and status in the colonial administration. Sadly, we must acknowledge that the American Ceylon Mission's approach to education sparked an aggressively competitive response by the Tamil Hindu community that led to Tamil educational superiority in Sri Lanka, which in turn fomented a source of grievance with the Buddhist/Sinhalese community that fuelled ethnic tensions. This historic blindness, which confused the secular colonial ideology of progress with the Christian gospel, still weighs heavily on JDCSI through the actions of the United Church of Christ's (UCC) Global Ministries and Jaffna College Trustees, who cling blindly to their need for privilege and status in their dealings with us, and who continue to fund those like Paul's self-aggrandising 'super apostles' in the schismatic group. And as in Paul's day, this self-appointed group continues to cause violence and discord in JDCSI, as seen most recently in their unwarranted intervention in the appointment of a new Principal for Uduvil Girls' College.

But from today we are a national church raised up into Christ's new creation. So after this Council, I will write to the General Secretary of CSI and ask him to invite his equivalent in the UCC to convene a Reconciliation Working Group to begin a new conversation about strengthening relations between our two churches in general and with JDCSI in particular.

Paul again guides our path as reconcilers. Our Colleges are to become God's servants in their solidarity with those who have suffered injustice and violence, and our response is founded on 'speaking the truth' (6:7). The 'old things' where JDCSI's historic colleges provided education that became a pathway to privilege and status has passed. Indeed, this missiological misstep has reaped a bitter fruit for our Diocese, for so many of those who benefited by the privileged education system in Jaffna that was built on the foundations of missionaries have fled our country, and perhaps ironically, live now in the safety of those countries from which many of those missionaries first came. The 'old things' have passed away quite literally. But as Christ's new creation, we are now living in new relationship with those who share our passion for the educational advancement of all young people in Sri Lanka, whether Christian, Hindu or Buddhist. This calling to our Diocese is what the establishment of the Centre of Excellence for Reconciliation Studies at Jaffna College was set up to address. Again Paul exhorts us: 'we urge you also not to accept the grace of God in vain. ···See, now is the acceptable time; see, now is the day of salvation!' (6:1-2b). Today I call on members of Council with a passion for personal, community and national reconciliation through education to make known your passion to your Bishop, the JDCSI Secretary, or the Centre Chairperson, Rev. Sanjeewa Weerarathna. As Christ's ambassadors for reconciliation, let us find a way to show forth this new ministry.

But Paul's focus is not on these 'old things'. It is enough for us to know that the time of these transgressions has passed and we are living in a new age. This is Paul's and our focus, to discern the true character of authentic ministry and mission. 'Ostentatious and extravagant displays of personal strengths have led the Corinthians to the mistaken conclusion that the essence of ministry consists of power and might. While authentic ministry does involve power and might, they are *God's* not the minister's',[1] or the Diocese's, or missionaries, or those who hold the purse strings of wealth and privilege.

The real focus for our mission today is to be characterized, not by power, but by vulnerability and weakness, for it is through our weakness that we have been blessed by the Spirit to rely totally on God's grace. So Paul's challenge for us today is to live as ambassadors of the reconciliation Christ has entrusted us with so that God's appeal may be made through us. In the same way that Paul wants the Corinthians to turn away from his opponents, and be reconciled to him, today I appeal to you to turn away from all those forces that destroy life or rob people of life. I appeal to you to turn away from all those who by their pursuit of power and might seek to divide our Diocese. As Paul focused on urging the Corinthian church to be reconciled to him, so today I urge you all to be reconciled to your Bishop.

Now, what do I mean when I urge you to be reconciled to your Bishop? Paul has a very clear meaning when he urges the Corinthians to be reconciled to him. For Paul and for me, our reconciliation in Christ starts with our shared suffering. I stand with Paul when he says, 'But we have this treasure in clay jars, so that it may be made clear that this extraordinary power belongs to God and does not come from us. We are afflicted in every way, but not crushed; perplexed, but not driven to despair; persecuted, but not forsaken; struck down, but not destroyed; always carrying in the body the death of Jesus, so that the life of Jesus may also be made visible in our bodies' (5$^{:7-10}$).

---

[1] S. Wan, *Power in Weakness: conflict and rhetoric in Pau's second letter to the Corinthians*, Trinity Press International, Pennsylvania, 2000, p.57.

To you my friends and colleagues in ministry I wish to say that when you look at me as your Bishop, I pray that you see me, not as a figure of power and might, but one who is vulnerable and weak like a clay pot. For like Paul I know my weakness from experiences of persecution, violent opposition and being near death. When you have trouble and are facing difficulty, I urge you to see my solidarity with you in human suffering, so that together we may wait upon God's strength to help us find a way forward with your difficulties.

It has grieved me terribly since we last met in Council that pastors who have been caught up in trouble and difficulty have hidden their circumstance from me. I am saddened when I hear of pastors criticizing their sisters and brothers in Christ because they believe another pastor has been given a favor or special privilege by me. And it causes great hurt to me and our Diocese when pastors or congregations react to decisions with which they feel aggrieved by speaking violently or abusively about their concerns. Will not I, to whom God has shown abundant and life-giving mercy, now show mercy to any of my pastors and congregations in your time of trouble and despair? This is what God has equipped me for when he led me through manifold times of suffering and violence.

Paul puts my conviction about how together we are ambassadors for Christ's ministry of reconciliation when he says, 'as we have been given mercy, we do not lose heart, but we renounce the hidden things of shame, not behaving in craftiness or falsifying the word of God, but in openness of truth recommending ourselves to every human conscience before God' ($4^{:1-2}$). We are reconciled in Christ by his share in our suffering, and as reconciled people we are joined together through God's resurrection life to continue to struggle together in truth as we seek to embody Christ's new creation. Being reconciled to your Bishop does not mean the

Diocese can meet every human need. But it does mean that the concerns you entrust to me will be met with honesty and openness, and that in our shared weakness, we may open our hearts to receive God's strength and wisdom (4:6).

Paul's call to the church to take up the ministry of reconciliation as ambassadors of Christ can have no better starting place for us, no better ground for learning together how to exercise this ministry as a Diocese, than at the heart of our polity as a Diocese of the Church of South India. As we begin to live together as Christ's new creation as a national church called to minister reconciliation to our war-weary nation, the integrity of our message will be revealed to the nation by how we live together as loved and forgiven people who are now living together reconciled and reconciling lives, which have been transformed by God's life-giving mercy. The authentic nature of our Christian mission and ministry will first and foremost be shown by how we live together, pray together, and relate to each other in love.

So, as we live into our reconciled lives as Christ's new creation, our view of who we are, whom we have been, and whom we are called and gifted to be will change. As Paul says, 'from this moment on, therefore, we don't regard anybody from a merely human point of view' (5:16). We will see the world in its desperate need for Christ's reconciling love with new eyes. And we will see that what we are called to be as a national church charged to be ambassadors for Christ's ministry of reconciliation has involved a radical break with the traditions of an historical Tamil church.

So what is the view from where we are today at the birth of this national, reconciled church? There was a time when all our Diocese's dreams of Christ's saving grace were concentrated on the 'merely human' ideals of Tamil nationalism. But Christ's death and resurrection mean all such dreams must come to dust,[2] for in Christ's new creation, 'God was reconciling the world to himself' (5:19). At our Eucharist for this Council meeting, let us give thanks on the 200th anniversary of their arrival in our country for the faith of ACM leaders who sacrificed the church they had nurtured under God and freely gave it to the Tamil church established as the Jaffna Diocese of the Church of South India. Let us rejoice at the faith of our forebears in that Tamil Church, giving thanks to God for their wise leadership and sacrificial service. Let us grieve what has now passed away, confessing our sadness at so much that has been familiar and comforting is now no more. And let us wait with Christ in faith that our suffering and death is known by God and that God has this day raised us to new life with our being a national church.

For our church has today entered the world of our national life, which has now been reconciled to God's self. Now we are called to implement that reconciliation, to put it into effect. God is 'entrusting the message of reconciliation to us' (5:19). So something new has happened to JDCSI, and now something new must happen.

But what is the concrete reality of this new creation into which we have been blessed? Paul shows us a model for how God's new creation comes to fruition. In chapter six, he lists many of the hardships he has endured and the gifts of grace with which God has blessed God's servants in the midst of suffering, difficulties and violence. For myself, I have endured two attempts on my life, been vilified and slandered by enemies in the church, and suffered betrayals and corrupt behaviour that has plundered our church.

---

[2] N.T. Wright, *Paul for Everyone: 2 Corinthians*, Westminster John Knox Press, Louisville Kentucky, 2004, p. 64.

Yet I will say with Paul that in the midst of these hardship I have been blessed 'by purity, knowledge, patience, kindness, holiness of spirit, genuine love, truthful speech, and the power of God' (6:6-7). I have been taught to respond to sin and evil through the power of God's reconciling love. For me, this is genuinely new in my life. Also, without the example of Paul, I would not open my heart to you with these truths. For Paul shows us how to be vulnerable and open-hearted in a world that knows and trusts more of the ways of violence and greed than it knows and trusts God's love.

I commend to you Paul's example, for as we trust God to be with us in our vulnerability of being open-hearted with our neighbors and communities, those amongst whom we minister will receive the experience of God's love. For when 'we are ambassadors for Christ, (it is) God (who) is making his appeal through us' (5:20). And when people experience God's love speaking to them through us, that love will reconcile them to God and to us. To support our pastors in practicing vulnerability and open-heartedness in their pastoral work, I have requested the Director of our Centre for Holistic Healing (CHH) to conduct a series of two-day workshops on pastoral listening for pastors in the key regions of the Diocese over the next two years. I commend these workshops to all our pastors, and look forward to the developing solidarity amongst our pastors as you strengthen your trust in Christ's presence in your struggles that will equip you further to be in solidarity with the pain and struggles of our people.

Here is the truth of how the miracle of reconciliation takes place. Christ says, "'My grace is sufficient for you, for power is made perfect in weakness." So, I will boast all the more gladly of my weaknesses, so that the power of Christ may dwell in me' (12:9). When you allow yourself to meet others with your vulnerability, trusting in God for your strength, you trust the ones you meet to trust you and God with their weakness. Christ's reconciling mercy springs from our solidarity with Christ's weakness on the cross, for when we are 'in Christ' in his suffering, God is with us in resurrection power and life.

Paul's wisdom here has encouraged me to request our Diocese's lay training committee to organise a 'Healing of Memories' workshop run by our Anglican friends for lay leaders across our Diocese. These workshops provide a safe space for lay participation in learning to tell the story of your life, so that painful memories may be brought into the light and healing mercy of God's love made present in the learning community. I commend this opportunity for training for all those lay members of Council who hear today Christ's call on your life to be an ambassador for Christ's ministry of reconciliation. We need to equip one another for the new ways of living that come from being Christ's new creation.

Paul also recognizes in his second letter to the Corinthians that equipping one another for new ways of living into the grace of Christ's new creation will require the exercise of spiritual discipline. He leaves dealing with this matter until the end of his epistle, and so I will conclude my charge to this Council meeting with a call to strengthen the exercise of spiritual discipline in our Diocese. After exhorting the congregation at Corinth to be reconciled to him, Paul acknowledges that there are still disruptive and divisive elements in the church. There is still 'quarrelling, jealousy, anger, selfishness, slander, gossip, conceit, and disorder' (12:20). I am disturbed that some pastors do not follow our guidelines for handling church offerings, others have ventured off into ways of earning money beyond their stipends, and some congregations feel disempowered, confused and frustrated by the behaviour of their pastors.

As Bishop, my first response is to welcome both pastors and congregations who are confused about what is appropriate behaviour in a national church with a ministry of reconciliation. I repeat what I said earlier, that I desire to be reconciled with all in my Diocese. But so there is no misunderstanding, I will draw your attention to a fixed point that we will need to come to in any such conversations. Following Paul, I will enquire of you, 'Examine yourselves to see whether you are living in the faith.' (13:5a). Paul's enquiry is established on your need to be reconciled to God in Christ. And so I will enquire in like manner. 'Test yourselves. Do you not realize that Jesus Christ is in you?—unless, indeed, you fail to meet the test!' (13:5b).

You may only be reconciled to your Bishop if you are first reconciled to Christ. And so that is the test. I will desire to discern whether you are in fact in right relationship with our Lord. In the early church, the apostles were both judge and jury in such matters of spiritual discipline, but that is not the same circumstance for a Bishop of the Church of South India (CSI). In the next three months I will codify the information about spiritual and pastoral discipline provided for by CSI, and I will consolidate this into one code of spiritual and pastoral discipline for pastors and another for church members. I will consult with my pastors before finalizing the code for pastors and I will consult with the Diocesan Executive before finalizing the code for church members. It is my intention that each of these codes will offer support for individuals to repent and turn away from divisive and disruptive behaviour, while making it clear that an unrepented sin against Christ brings its own judgment of exclusion from the church. Paul's commitment to Christ's new creation is unequivocally merciful: 'For we cannot do anything against the truth, but only for the truth. For we rejoice when we are weak and you are strong. This is what we pray for, that you may become perfect ($13^{:8-9}$).

I commit myself to humbly follow the apostle's wise counsel, so that the new creation we are as a national church may always give glory to God.

'The grace of the Lord Jesus Christ, the love of God, and the communion of the Holy Spirit be with all of you' ($13^{:13}$).

And What does the Lord Require of you?

65th Session: Jaffna Diocesan Council of the Church of South India 2019

'He has shown you, O mortal, what is good. And what does the Lord require of you? To act justly and to love mercy and to walk humbly with your God.' Micah 6:8

Introduction

Dear Sisters and Brothers in Christ,

I stand before you to as your bishop to begin my seventh and likely final charge, filled with gratitude for God's faithfulness. As I look back to my first charge I recall that I stood in the same place, with a heart filled with thanksgiving for God's faithfulness. For God's faithfulness has been my rock and my strength. My heart is filled with gratitude for God's enduring love for our Church, the Church of South India, for this diocese, the Jaffna Diocese, for the faithful cloud of witnesses who surround us, and for God's love made manifest in our Council through each one of you.

When I stood before you in 2007, God's faithfulness to me as your bishop called me to charge you with the theme 'Journeying Together'. I trusted that God was calling me to be in solidarity with our diocese as we absorbed the painful reality of schism and shuddered under the ever louder guns and bombs of war. My trust was in the Book of Hebrews good news, "We are not among those who shrink back and so are lost, but among those who move forward and so are saved" (10:[39]). I called you to journey with me, trusting that God's will was for us to journey onward amidst various trials, temptations, obstacles and turbulence.

I am so grateful that God's unbounded faithfulness to us has led us through the many days of darkness on our journey together. And now today, it is time for me to recognize that my days as your Bishop are drawing to their conclusion. Next time this Council meets under God's grace in three years' time, you will have a new Bishop. In this charge I wish to look back over the journey we have shared, and also look forward to the future which awaits us.

Over the next three years, we will make preparations to journey in different directions. Now, once again, the faithfulness of God which filled my heart in 2007 fills my heart as we face the future, each in our own ways. Perhaps the main difference in these two occasions is that in 2007, God's faithfulness drew us together in our journey of faith and witness, whereas today God calls us to reflect on our journey with a question about how to face our diverging futures: 'And what does the Lord require of you?' (Micah 6:[8]) Let us listen to how this question speaks to us individually and collectively.

God's judgment and salvation

The prophet Micah frames this question by looking back over Israel's painful past as a war-torn nation. This is important for the question reveals his faith in God's purposes. Looking back in time, Micah discerns the hand of God's severe judgment on his people. But it is only after God's people hear God's judgment on their past behaviour as a war-torn nation overwhelmed by violence and death that they are able to hear the good news of God's life-giving salvation. With Micah's prophetic imagination as our guide, let us then open our hearts and minds to hear God's word of judgment and salvation. I am convinced that it is only as we open our hearts to the fullness of God's word that we may know with grateful hearts the richness of God's faithfulness to JDCSI through the trials of our journey together.

Micah's question is answered with a word that sets out the future direction for God's people. These words provide the text for my charge. 'He has shown you, O mortal, what is good. ... To act justly and to love mercy and to walk humbly with your God.' (Micah 6:8) Micah's question and answer comes three-quarters of the way through the short book that bears his name. So first I will explain how Micah arrives at this question, before looking closely at the future he is called to announce to God's people.

The name 'Micah' means 'Who is like the Lord?' The prophet's name expresses both wonder and praise at the incomparable God of Israel. This confident shout of wonder is both the first word and the last word (1:1-4; 7:18) in the Book of Micah. These words resonate deeply with me today, as I give thanks for the faithfulness of God that was there at the beginning of my bishopric and is still with me. There is another resonance in having a name that recalls the liberating power of God. I give thanks that I was named 'Daniel' by my parents, in honor of the Revd. D.T. Niles, who carried the torch for the liberating power of the gospel in ecumenical circles both in Ceylon/Sri Lanka and in the turbulent days of the post-world war years. Knowing my Biblical name also strengthened me like the great prophet Daniel was strengthened to witness to God's justice when he was living under foreign occupation.

At first it may be difficult to reconcile Micah's praise for God because so much of this book is filled with page after page of God's anger. For God's judgment is deeply passionate against those who, through their persistent and wanton acts of injustice, defiled the covenant God made with Israel. Perhaps the acclamation 'Who is like the Lord?' is also a cry of desperation. 'Who is like the Lord?' No one!'[1] There have been many occasions during my bishopric when I have felt overwhelmed by the injustice facing our diocese and I echoed Micah's lament.

Perhaps Micah's courage to speak the truth about God's searing judgment against people who perpetrated injustice was due to his unwavering trust in God's salvation – God's mercy? I will say more about this later, but Micah's promise that God will gather a faithful remnant (2^{12}) is a saving grace for all who are at times overwhelmed by the world's evil. I am grateful beyond words for all those loyal people who God chose to stand with me in the face of the purifying fire of God's judgment, and who showed me God's great mercy. In gratitude I think of my wife Thaya and daughter Gita, I remember the 'unknown' young female doctor who jumped into the ambulance at Marawilla hospital to accompany me to the General Hospital, Colombo after the assassination attempt; Dr Irene Sathiaseelan, Dr Araiaranee Gnanathasan, Sumanthiran, Nagalingam, and Rev. Pathmathayalan who all ministered to me in their own way when I was near death; the first Bishop's

---

[1] S. Dempster, *Micah*. 2019. William B. Eerdmans Publishing Company, Grand Rapids, Michigan (e-book).

secretary Mr CD Chinnakone, and first Bishop's Chaplain Rev. S. Ariaratnam in the midst of betrayal and schism, and Mrs. Leela Ratnam for being a constant prayer companion. God's goodness in gathering a faithful remnant is life-giving.

The task of confronting the nations of Judah and Israel with their overwhelming sin and evil was a test of faith and courage for Micah. Micah declared that God's people had turned away from God and no-one was practicing justice ($7^{:1-2}$). Now they must bear God's anger for the injustices they have perpetrated. Micah was not afraid to speak the plain truth about people who abused their position for profit ($2^{:1-5}$); who used their religion to justify their abuse ($2^{:6-11}$); and to tell the religious leaders that their temple would crumble to dust because of their corrupt exploitation of their religious privileges ($3^{:9-12}$). Micah's list of injustices strikes a chord with our diocese's experience from the time we began our journey together.

Micah's message of judgment is in three parts: first, the whole world must hear God's word ($1^{:2}$); then the religious leaders of Israel are called to account ($3^{:1}$); and then all the people of Israel are called to hear this word ($6^{:1-2}$). Our nation, our religious leaders and then all people are also all addressed by the prophet's three part word of judgment, even as we Sri Lankans seem to be in constant, seemingly never ending conflict about whose fault it was for a particular hurt. We have spent decades and maybe longer shifting the blame for war and violence onto an Other, fighting about who was here first, or who fired the first shot, or whose religion better speaks the truth, or which community has suffered the most at the hands of the others. Micah is not interested in deciding the cause of who is to blame. Micah declares that God's judgment is aimed at those who have broken the covenant with God. God's judgment is against those who have sinned against

God's Word. And no-one, - the national leaders, the religious establishment or the people themselves - can escape this judgment.

Judgment for the world

Micah first word of judgment addresses the whole world. All nations need to hear God's word ($1^{:2}$) because God's judgment is against God's chosen people and the respective capital cities of the northern kingdom of Israel and the southern kingdom of Judah ($1^{:5}$). Why would God turn against the capital cities of Jerusalem and Samaria? It is horrifying for the Israelites to be confronted with the prophetic judgment against their beloved cities. But Micah's announcement of the sins of Samaria and Jerusalem means no one else is to blame for their plight. The national political leadership has sinned against God's sovereign rule.

The national leaders in the two capital cities are guilty of idolatry, trusting in their own strength with no regard for the Lord. They practice robbery, dishonesty, deceit, and violence ($6^{:9-12}$). Their actions lead to social ruin ($7^{:1-6}$). It is as if God had announced judgment against both Colombo and Kilinochchi, that is, the southern capital of the Sri Lankan state government and the northern capital of the Liberation Tigers of Tamil Eelam (LTTE). And when I listen to Micah's description of how the two kingdoms have sinned against God's covenant with God's people, like Micah I lament as I feel the force of God's judgment falling on our situation. The purpose of God's judgment is to force us to look in the mirror and know our need for repentance. For we are identified with Jerusalem and Samaria, and so we must conclude the prophet's judgment also falls upon us: 'God's people are not without sin'.[2]

---

[2] L. Stulman and H Kim, *You are my People: an introduction to Prophetic Literature.* Abingdon Press, Nashville. 2010. p. 211.

What follows is an indescribable surprise. Micah announces that in God's mercy, the good Shepherd will free the cities from their captivity to sin by breaking down their walls to liberate a remnant, with the Lord, the good Shepherd 'at their head' ($2^{:12\text{-}13}$). Let me offer you a vision for our cities and our nation based on our Diocesan Council's initiative several years ago to gather together Hindu, Buddhist, Muslim and other Christian leaders for a multi-faith ceremony on the International Remembrance Day (11 November). Let us give our Kilinochchi and Colombo churches a new name and a new purpose as Peace Memorial Churches, and dedicate them to this vision in the name of JDCSI on International Remembrance Day with a multi-faith ceremony, one in each of the following two years. As the Lord gathered in the victims of injustice in Micah's day, so let us imagine a new future of peace-making and healing where the Diocesan Council commits us to turning away from leaders who use their power to oppress bodies, and imprison minds and souls. Having survived the long years of national darkness, shall we now witness to the light that has come amongst us in Jesus Christ? (see John $1^{:3b\text{-}5}$).

Judgment for religious leaders

From the national and world view, Micah then turns his attention to the religious leadership. Micah's judgment is unequivocal. The religious leaders have gradually removed God from the centre of their lives to the point they no longer pay any attention to God's justice. The result is that they no longer minister justice to the poor and oppressed in their society. 'Listen, you heads of Jacob and rulers of the house of Israel! Should you not know justice? - you who hate the good and love the evil' ($3^{:1\text{-}2a}$). To hide their injustice, the religious leaders justified themselves, saying that their evil is for the good.

Micah's detail of God's judgment is scathing. Micah tells of religious leaders responsible for fostering justice who have used their position for personal gain at the expense of the poor ($3^{:2\text{-}3}$). Prophets have spoken falsely of 'God's peace' to curry favour with those in power ($3^{:5}$), and political leaders, prophets and priests have conspired together to build their special projects and the Temple on oppressive labour practices and corruption, while preaching that they are doing God's will ($3^{:9\text{-}11}$). Because of this shocking idolatry, God terminates their building project. Jerusalem and its temple will be turned to rubble ($3^{:12}$).

Surely Micah's uncompromising word of judgment shines a light on the behaviour of those who led the 2006 schismatics that broke from JDCSI. But it also shines a light on our Diocese. I confess before God that our Diocese was guilty of providing cover to a pastor who used the good name of the Diocese to market his mission for his personal financial gain. We allowed the plight of orphans in Diocesan care to become a front for his accumulation of funds from international aid and church agencies. We seemed not to notice when he took on the trappings of wealth; when he used his status as a man of God to hide his corrupting schemes and to entice others from home and abroad to finance his projects. And he exploited vulnerable women and children. It is a devastating truth that all of this was taking place while he was a pastor in our Diocese. So when God's terminating judgment broke into our being through the 2006 schism, the Diocese as we knew it came to a crashing end.

The prophet Isaiah likens God's devastating judgment to being both purified and tested in a fiery furnace. 'I will turn my hand against you; I will smelt away your dross as with lye and remove all your alloy' (Is.$1^{:25}$), and 'see, I have refined you, but not like silver; I have tested you in the furnace of adversity' (Is.$48^{:10}$).

Isaiah recognised that bearing God's judgment may bring great adversity, and this is true of the impact of the schism on our Diocese. But the prophetic imagination points to two profound truths. First, God's judgment smelts away dross, and second, it produces a better metal, refined and tested. Micah's preaching is an unmistakable call to repentance to political leaders, prophets and priests.

In 2015, my charge emphasized repentance is absolutely central to Jesus' ministry. *Metanoia*, or a 'change of heart' is the only fitting response to Christ's call to live the will of God. The particular emphasis that Jesus gave to the concept of repentance was the radical meaning of 'to turn around.' It involved a profound alteration of the course and direction of one's life, its motivations and objectives. Following the schism, the Bishop's house welcomed people of all castes at the front door. The Diocesan Council has worked strongly with pastors and treasurers to properly account for all funds, including new constitutional safeguards, and has adopted policies and encouraged staff training for child safe practices in Diocesan institutions. But perhaps the most radical change was changing from being a national Tamil Diocese and turning towards becoming a nationally reconciled and reconciling Diocese of Sinhalese and Tamil peoples.

Micah announces what this radical turning to God and God's justice and peace means. 'In days to come ... many nations shall come and say: "Come, let us go up to the mountain of the Lord, to the house of the God of Jacob; that he may teach us his ways and that we may walk in his paths. ... He shall judge between many peoples, and shall arbitrate between strong nations far away; they shall beat their swords into ploughshares, and their spears into pruning-hooks; nation shall not lift up sword against nation, neither shall they learn war anymore; but they shall all sit under their own vines and under their own fig trees, and no one shall make them afraid; for the mouth of the Lord of hosts has spoken"' ($4^{:1,2-4}$). The God of our salvation has fulfilled Micah's prophetic promise in our midst, for we are now judged by God to be joined as peace-makers. We are no longer separate peoples defined by enmity. This is God's will for us made possible by our purification through God's smelting fire. I charge you to take hold of God's promise of wellbeing made manifest in our Diocese for the sake of the peoples of Sri Lanka, so that we may be freed at last from our past captivity to coveting land and possessions, and being fearful of the other.

This past year I have received several approaches from the leaders of the schismatics through various third parties. So far I have not responded, because these approaches have all been characterized by their appeal to what appears to be the furthering of their own interests. St. Paul warns against those who are covetous, declaring that 'no one who is greedy (that is, an idolater), has any inheritance in the kingdom of Christ and of God' (Ephesians $5^{:5}$). So without their disclosure of their experience of God's judgment and testimony of repentance for the sin of schism, their covetous spirit places them outside our fellowship. The Diocese we have become today as a national reconciled and reconciling Church is not the Diocese the schismatics broke away from. Our future is as a Diocese that has been smelted and purified by God's judgment. 'For all the peoples walk, each in the name of its god, but we will walk in the name of the Lord our God' ($4^{:5}$). I rejoice in the journey in which JDCSI has been led by the Spirit of Christ, for we have been transformed to walk the path of God's justice, mercy and peace. It is to walk on a journey sustained by God's guidance, God's presence, God's hands in and through us. So I can testify with St. Paul: 'I can do all things through him who strengthens me' (Philippians 4:13). May the Lord continue to lead this Diocese on the path of Christ's justice, mercy and peace.

The people are called to account

Finally, after God's judgment against the cities and nations, then the religious leaders, Micah calls the people of Israel to account. The judgment is short and sharp. The people's worship of God has become preoccupied with external displays of their own virtue. Their worship has forgotten that God first liberated Israel from slavery in Egypt. Instead, the people's worship has become a new form of slavery focussed on being a religious performance that will prove their worth by their own efforts (6:3-7). And it is here that Micah arrives at the question which is the theme for this Council meeting: 'And what does the Lord require of you?' To understand the deeper meaning of this question, we need to understand God's sorrow and disappointment that Israel cannot see all that God has done for them. God's heart is troubled. Yes, the people have forgotten their liberation from slavery in Egypt. They no longer remember the generations of God's constant faithfulness to the covenant promises of comfort and wellbeing. In all of this 'He has shown you, O mortal, what is good' (6:8a).

So how should we now worship God? God answers this question through Micah's prophetic word: 'To act justly and to love mercy and to walk humbly with your God' (6:8b). Two things are immediately important. One, true worship focusses on just and merciful relationships offered humbly to God and neighbour. Justice, loving mercy, and walking with God are all to do with relationships - that is, they each describe the quality of a relationship. And two, doing justice and mercy in our relationships with God and neighbour relies upon the qualities of justice and loving mercy being fully inter-connected for them to be fruitfully implemented.

Today I thank God for all who have worked for justice for the Diocese in the courts, especially our legal consultants led by Sumanthiran. All have sincerely and with loving kindness extended their support to uphold the Bishop. Following the initiative of our Secretary, I am delighted to advise Council that Sumanthiran has accepted our invitation to continue his support for the Diocese after my retirement. Justice, mercy and humility before God are present with us, by God's grace. Then I remember the fearless journalist Victor Karunairajan whom God sent at a time of perplexity. Victor's writings called for justice against false prophets, and with helpful clarity exposed the injustices they provoked. He too upheld justice with loving kindness in humble service to God.

I rejoice at those who joined themselves to the Diocese in loving mercy to strengthen our ministry of mercy and justice. For many dear friends, particularly John and Marg who came into our lives and then walked humbly with God and us, giving support spiritually, psychologically, economically, scholarly and educationally. My siblings have showered me with God's mercy, particularly my eldest sister, Esther Shanti, who filled in the place of my mother, and my younger brother, Gunalan, who sustained me in my struggles. In the blessings of justice and mercy conferred upon me and on our diocese, we have learned what it means to walk humbly with our God.

When I have been ministered to by those who walk humbly with God, I have learned again how to live in the image of God, who loves justice and mercy. Proper worship leads to becoming more like God in justice and mercy. Not only will you be empowered to live life in spirit and truth, but you will also be a living witness to the glory of God. For 'we have this treasure in clay jars, so that it may be made clear that this extraordinary power belongs to God and does not come from us' (2 Cor. 4:7).

This brings me to my final point. According to Walter Brueggemann, worship that brings us humbly before God to be made and re-made in God's image, needs the support and guidance of disciplined theological reflection. Brueggemann says, 'Perhaps we have no more important theological investigation than to discern in whose image we have been made.'[3] I am so grateful for the opportunities I have received during my bishopric to grow theologically and to be formed in my faith by attending national, Asian and world level conferences, consultations and seminars. It has been a joy and a privilege to present papers and interact with ordained and lay scholars and church members for the strengthening and development of my faith as a member of the universal church.

Now, over the final three years of my term as bishop, I commit to strengthening the faith and theological wisdom of my clergy and the Diocesan Council. There are many challenges ahead of you, and appropriate forms of theological education and formation will help to build your strengths and creativity to take up the challenges in three areas in particular.

One is the need for a servant leadership faith and development program. This will be a high level commitment for a small number of clergy and lay leaders in Diocesan institutions, to receive an extended program in governance, management, finance, property, pastoral care and theological integration. I am charging the Board of Ministerial Workers to work with me to develop the program, recruit and select the participants, and evaluate the program.

---

[3] W. Brueggemann, *The Prophetic Imagination,* Minneapolis: Fortress. 2001, p.17.

Second is a Women's Theology Seminar for women clergy and members of the Diocesan Council. The Seminar will provide regular opportunities for women members to meet together for theological reflection, encourage women's voices in the business of the Diocese, and encourage practical action on injustices facing women in Sri Lanka and our Diocese. I am charging the Board for Women's Work to work with me to develop and implement the program. I will have further details about these two proposals further in our Council meeting.

Third is an invitation to pastors who are working in both parish ministry and paid secular work and others who may feel called to ministry in secular work to meet with me individually or in small groups to discuss what this means for their vocation, their accountability to the Bishop, and their commitment to the common good. I remind the Council that my much-loved brother Gunalan maintained his business interests while faithfully serving the Diocese, to the benefit of us all. I believe it is incumbent on the Council to understand this development amongst us, and to discern whether God is calling the Church to new forms of serving justice and loving kindness. I invite you who sense a calling in this sphere of God's mission to begin the conversation with me.

I have three more years of service as your bishop – in that time I pray we will grow in wisdom, cooperation, creativity and joy. In particular, may you all be charged with the spirit of Micah's prophetic imagination until you are more fully made in God's image and know more closely God's character of justice and mercy. Then when the day of parting comes, we may each rejoice in the faithfulness of God, affirming: 'But as for me, I will look to the Lord, I will wait for the God of my salvation; my God will hear me.' (7:7)

www.ingramcontent.com/pod-product-compliance
Lightning Source LLC
Chambersburg PA
CBHW021004180726
47993CB00017B/775